Collecting Information with a Passion

by Corey Lowe

Dorrance Publishing Co
585 Alpha Drive
Pittsburgh, PA 15238
Visit our website at *www.dorrancebookstore.com*

ISBN: 979-8-8892-5203-0
eISBN: 979-8-8892-5703-5

The most effective weapon a human being can have in his or her arsenal is information. You might be thinking of a gun, knife, or something more modern like a computer. It is true that if you have a computer, you can do just about anything. From taking someone's identity to hacking NASA, not saying you should do that, just making a point. A computer, however, is useless without the information needed to do whatever you need it to do. From the beginning of time, information has always played an important role from the moment we're born. Even animals from dinosaurs to today's animals use information to get what they want. Whether it was the outcome of a major battle or even down to simple revenge, it was always down to the right information. The use of information has two sides to it, good intel and bad intel. Now these two sides all boil down to how you use it. You have to be very careful because the slightest mistake just might cost you everything. You might think I'm over analyzing the importance of information, but trust me, information can and has killed. Your opinion may vary but let me show you why information is still the deadliest weapon a person can use.

"Keep both eyes open… Clear your mind… Focus… Breathe… Take a deep breath… Squeeze the trigger, don't pull it."

(Loud gunshot)

"Damn. Right through the middle Rakes. Turns out you're a natural with a rifle."

Rakes smiles, "Thanks Keys, my gun recertification is coming up in a few weeks, so I appreciated you for being my spot. The lieutenant recommended me for the counter sniper unit, so I have to bring my A game."

Keys smiles. "So, it is true, you're leaving the team?"

Rakes smiles and sighs. "Just keeping my options open and it'll just be a substitution thing, so let's not get ahead of ourselves. So, do you want to give it a go with the rifle, Keys? Think you can hit my mark?"

Keys chuckles, "I think I'll pass. I really don't do guns."

"What's the matter? Don't tell me Hank Keys is… dare I say… scared?"

Keys scoffs and smiles. "Not at all, you should know me by now, I prefer the blade over a gun anytime. What… don't look at me like that. Something on your mind?"

Rakes side-smiles. "Nothing… I'll just chalk it up there with your thing that you do."

(Ring Ring)

"Detective Rakes… yeah ok, we'll be there in few. That was the lieutenant…he wants us back at the district. You up for it?"

"It's been two months Rakes, Lieutenant already signed off on my return after everything that went down. Even then, he forced me to take more time.

It wasn't in the cards for me; besides I was losing my mind after the first week. So yeah, let's do this."

Rakes scoffs and smiles. "Don't know why I'm not surprised… alright, you drive. Hey, what we got?"

Gamble scoffs, "Look at you, not even a hey, just itching to get back in it."

"What can I say Gamble? Might be a little messed up, but solving a murder is what I need to get back in."

"That's more than a little messed up Keys."

Keys hesitates, "Yeah, I can see that… you know what I mean, can we get back to the case?"

Lieutenant sighs, "There's no case. Alright, listen up, I need you three to go to pier 66 for recertification. As you all know it's required every three years, so I don't want to hear it."

Gamble angrily sighs, "C'mon Lieutenant, don't you think this is a little crazy? Why is this even a requirement? It's almost like they're saying we don't know how to do our jobs."

Rakes smiles "Can't believe I'm saying this, but I actually agree with Gamble. It's almost an insult. What about you, Keys? Don't you think this is unnecessary?"

Keys sighs. "I can see both sides. I mean everyone can use a refresher every now and then, but in the long run it can be a little insulting."

Gamble scoffs) "I was wondering why it was so hot today, Hank. Keys is agreeing with me."

Lieutenant clears his throat) "While I enjoy your opinions, the recertifications are required to continue being detectives. So, if you refuse, then there's the door. Knowing you would complain, I did however make a request, or more likely a request was made, and I accepted it. You will not only participate in the training course but you're going to teach it."

Rakes stares with confusion) "Teach it? What do you mean?"

"It's pretty self-explanatory Rakes, you four are my best detectives here, so I arranged that you teach the new rookies. Is that a problem?"

Gamble scoffs, "Yeah, I say it is. That's even more insulting, not only do we have to take this course, but now we have to babysit rookies."

Rakes smiles, "Oh c'mon Gamble, you were a rookie once upon a time and by the way, it could be fun. So, what exactly will we be teaching Lieutenant?"

"I have no clue. It's whatever the instructor tells you. I figure that would make it interesting for you."

Rakes smiles, "Well, I can't disagree with that. Now I'm excited."

Lieutenant smiles, "You're awfully quiet. Are you sure you're up for this? You still got time?"

Keys cracks a smile, "Honestly Lieutenant, I guess we'll find out after this class."

"Alright you three, get going. Standing around is not going to get you re-certified. The instructor is waiting."

Keys looks around, "Where's Monroe?"

"Don't worry, your partner is already on scene. Good luck you three, and try to learn something… Rakes, keep your partner out of trouble, will you?"

Rakes smiles, "Always Lieutenant."

"Detective Keys… good to have you back and keep an eye on them for me…"

Keys smiles, "Copy that."

Gamble smirks, "You sure you're ready to get back in the fray, Keys? I have to be honest, I've enjoyed the quiet since you were on leave."

Keys smiles. "I haven't even had my coffee yet and you and me are already here."

Gamble smiles and scoffs. "Don't take it personal, it was a compliment after all. Rakes, Monroe, and I have been solving cases like crazy. And to make it sweeter, we didn't even need your stupid, annoying little thing you always do."

Rakes chuckles. "Which is code for he tried doing it but failed horribly."

"Actually, to be fair we all tried it. But neither one of us could pull it off."

Gamble grunts, "Great, nice going, Rakes. Now he's going to have a bigger head then normal."

Keys smiles. "Oh, c'mon Gamble, you should know me better than that. I mean after all, some people got it, and some people don't. It's all good."

Gamble scoffs. "You see what you done started, Rakes? It's going to be a long day."

Rakes smiles, "Sorry partner… we're here."

"Took you guys long enough. I've been going crazy."

Keys sighs, "It's not even noon yet and you already have that look, Monroe? Can we have at least a good morning?"

Monroe stares at Keys, "I don't know yet. Do you have something for me?"

"Humph, do we have something for her Rakes?"

Rakes smiles. "One large coffee with three pumps of vanilla and a cup of sugar with light whipped cream."

"That's what took us so long? Your complicated coffee order.. So you were saying?"

Monroe smiles. "Good morning my esteemed colleagues, today is going to be a long and rough day."

Gamble scoffs.

"Someone's not in her usual mood today."

"I take it you meant the new candidates? Not a fan of them, are you?"

"No, not yet. I just got here about an hour before you guys. Lieutenant already filled me in on the switch up. So now we're trainers?"

Gamble coughs, "Yeah, that's just about the gist of it. But you know the lieutenant, I'm pretty sure there's something else to it."

"Yeah, for once I agree with you, Gamble. But in any case, it should be fun."

Sgt. Williams yells, "Are you four done standing around over there? If you don't mind, can we begin!?"

Monroe sighs, "C'mon you three. Let's get this over with."

Rakes whispers to Keys, "What going on with your partner? Gamble's right with her mood; she seems preoccupied."

Keys stares, "Yeah, I noticed. But whatever it is, I'm sure she can handle it."

Sgt. Williams speaks, "Alright listen up, I'm sure your lieutenant told you we're switching up a little this go-around. In order to get your recertification, you will not be just taking the class, but teaching it. Before you get your panties in a bunch… Gamble… these five recruits behind me are the top cadets in their class. They cleared every obstacle thrown at them."

Gamble sucks his teeth. "That still doesn't take away from the matter that we have to play babysitter. They might be the best in their class, but the real world isn't some class, Sergeant."

"Well, that's what we're here for, aren't we Gamble? To teach them and get them ready. Don't forget we've all been here before at some point. We've all started as rookies and I'm pretty sure your trainers said the same thing about each and every one of you. You don't have to like it, but you will respect them, that is"if you want your recertification."

Gamble scoffs. "Copy that, Sergeant."

"Now on that note, this class is similar to your last recertification, but this go-around we're going to get a little more hands on."

"How so Sergeant?"

"I'll explain after the introductions, Rakes. Now, let's go meet your new friends. Alright everyone, gather 'round. We're burning time so I'm going to make this quick. Detectives meet your students; Daniel Channing, first in his class… nothing else needs to be said. Following him is Eric Cross, former security guard. A bit grounded, but gets the job done. Next up is Lisa Westwood, one of the best uncover officers we got. We were able to close three major drug cases with her. Next, we got Mr. Melvin Lowell, our top profiler. We were able to close that triple murder case few weeks ago with his help. He was the only one to figure out the murdered was a twin… crazy right? Last but not least, we have Sandra Ellis, anything you want to know about any weapons, and I do mean any weapon, ask her. Not only that, her knowledge on making any type of weapon is second to none."

Keys smiles. "I can already tell you had an interesting childhood. Nothing wrong with that."

Ellis blushes. "It's just a sort of a hobby, sir. It's nothing really."

Sergeant talks, "Alright recruits, listen up; these detectives behind me are the best detectives in the district. You might have heard of some of them, some you might not. With that in mind, if some of you are thinking negatively about certain detectives, keep it to yourself. These detectives are here to train and determine your capabilities for when or if you're in the field. This class is a reenactment of a crime scene. As you have already surmised, you work the scene, gather evidence, and solve the case. All you need to know about the case is here in the folder. This is not timed, but let's not drag this out. In all our cases, we've never rushed to solve them. In doing so, we tend to miss important details to the investigation. As I said before, this is not timed, but let's try and wrap this up in at least six hours. Your primary scene starts on that ship, from there you're on your own. Do we have any questions? Yes, Channing."

"Sir, is there a type of order for us to follow? Any rules we need to know?"

"Negative Channing, you five determine your own order and rules of doing things. The main purpose of this course is for you to determine each other strengths and weaknesses. Keep in mind this is just a class, so no sucking up and no showboating trying to outdo one another. But I expect my top recruits to give it their all… you either pass as a team or fail as a team… am I understood?"

The recruits all yell, "Yes sir!"

"As for you four, your recertifications determines their success. Don't get me wrong, your certification is guaranteed whether they pass or fail. But if our top detectives failed at training a few wet behind the ears rookies? Yeah, I don't think that would be a good look on your patches. Especially if you're gunning for promotion. With that in mind, no cheating… Gamble… This has to be done by the book... We got eyes everywhere watching this... So keep that in mind, I'm not the only one watching."

Gamble sucks his teeth. "C'mon Sergeant Give me a little credit."

Sergeant talks. "Alright, if there are no more questions, I'll leave you in the care of these fine detectives… Good luck kids."

Keys smiles. "Alright, this case isn't going to solve itself… after you."

Rakes chuckles. "So, are you guys nervous? I know I was. On my first day I was sweating bullets and choking on my words. It's ok to be nervous. Really no one? How about you Cross? Being former security, you must be used to this?"

"Oh no ma'am, I wouldn't say I'm used to it. I used to be security for the casino, but except on holidays when people get crazy, I barely did anything. Only thing that came close to this was my writing down descriptions from people who would steal. Being security just means a lot of walking and taking notes."

Rakes scoffs. "Ok first, if you call me 'ma'am' again, I'm going to shoot you in the shoulder. That goes for the rest of you, and second, I think being security gives you perspective. I mean in some ways, Cross, being security and being a cop are very similar, and not too many people are cut out for the job."

Cross smiles, "I'll keep that in mind Detective."

"Well, I'm not nervous, being a detective was always a dream of mine. Me I love puzzles, and it's always sort of a rush solving a challenging puzzle."

Keys smiles. "Is that right? And you are… Ellis… right? Another hobby of yours? Tell me something Ellis, why do you want to become a detective?"

Ellis sighs. "It's personal, but to sum it up I'm hard headed… much like puzzles, when I start something, I never quit… even if it takes years."

Keys smiles. "Humph, well ok, I expect to see that in all of you."

Channing whisper to Monroe. "Excuse me, this may not be my place, but we've all heard the rumors."

Monroe stares. "Let me stop you right there… Channing, was it? If there is anything you want to know about a certain someone, I suggest you should stop listening to rumors and just ask this someone yourself. And if you can't do that, then I suggest you take Sgt. Williams advice and keep your thoughts to yourself."

Channing sighs. "I meant no disrespect. I know he's your partner, Monroe. I only asked because even though I'm not in the army anymore, I'm still a soldier at heart and if I can't trust my teammate then…"

Monroe smiles. "If that's your concern Channing, then you got nothing to worry about. Out of everyone here, Hank Keys is the only one I'd trust my life with. And I'm not just saying that because he has saved my life once or twice before or because he's my partner. He has a unique attraction and a very annoying ability, but that's just me. Don't worry, I promise you by day ends you'll know what I'm talking about."

Gamble talks. "Alright, looks like we're here. They even secured the scene with police tape. Why bother? We're the only ones here, aren't we?"

"Easy partner, Sgt. Williams did say this year would be different. Guess they are going for a little more real than just a simulation? I don't know. What you think Monroe?"

"Well, it is different from the last time, Rakes, kind of creepy. Look at that, it looks like they're using a donor body for the victim instead of a mannequin. There are mannequins all around except the victim."

"You prefer them to be real bodies, Monroe?"

"Technically this one is real Gamble… I mean it's kind of messed up, right? I prefer mannequins if you ask me. But anyways, Sgt. Williams gave you six hours so get to it."

Rakes looks at Keys. "Alright you guys, walk us through it."

What goes through a person's mind after a certain trauma? Guess it all depends on what type of trauma it is. Some people are angry and distant… some go through depressions and flashbacks… and then there are those of us that that there is simply nothing going through their mind… nothing at all. Some just want to be left alone. May not make sense to some, but being left alone can sometime be the best medicine. But how does one truly get over a certain trauma? Do you ignore it, fight through it, or embrace it? In my personal opinion, there is just one right answer… D all the above, but like I said, it depends on the type. Trauma is a strong word, I guess… Who knows? Maybe it's just all in your head.

"What's wrong? What's with that look of shock you all have on your face? Snap out of it! I take it this is your first time seeing a dead body before? I'll take your silence as a yes. Not to be blunt, but if you can't handle this, then there's the door. Granted, this might be your first time seeing an actual body before, but we really don't have time to hold your hands."

Rakes sighs. "I know he can be intimidating and rude sometimes, but he's right in his own way. Now I will grant you all a little leeway being this is your first-time hands on, but like my partner said, you need to snap out of it. You guys said you were ready, right? So take a deep breath and get to it."

Monroe murmurs. "It would seem the sergeant misspoke about them being top cadets. When real life hits them they freeze up. Keys… They seem to be stuck."

Keys sighs, "Alright this doesn't count as helping, but I want to try something. I want you five to close your eyes, take a deep breath, and when I say open your eyes, we're going to give you the five questions we use when starting any case."

Rakes smiles. "I remember that all too well. This technique is very beneficial, and it does show results in the end."

Keys grins. "Alright everyone, close your eyes and take a deep breath and exhale through your nose. Now when I say open your eyes, each one of us will give you all a question and from there you five give us what you think the answer is. Keep in mind your answers are yours as a group, so whatever you decide as a group will determine if you chose the right answer. Ready… take a deep breath… exhale through your nose… now open your eyes!"

Monroe says, "Who? Who's the victim? Determining the who can help in the why your victim was killed."

Lowell takes a breath, "I don't see a purse or wallet so can't make a proper I.D. Upon first glance, victim is female, Caucasian, long brown hair, looks like late thirties, early forties."

Gamble grunts. "What the hell are you looking at us for? What do you want, a cookie or something? If you're seeking validation, then you're already starting off wrong. Is that all you have for a who? Alright then next question… what… what do you think or see that may have killed her? Keep in mind, sometimes things aren't what they appear."

Ellis clears her throat. "Jane Doe seems to have multiple lacerations on her face, arms, and wrist. Lying on the ground with glass shards all around from what looks like a struggle. First thought that pops in my head is I'm thinking an argument gone wrong; our victim gets into a heated argument and the killer pushes her into the glass table. The glass cuts the vein in her wrist and neck, and she bleeds out."

Cross stares. "That's one outcome or it could be poison."

"What makes you think poison, Cross?"

"Picture this; our victim here orders her meal as we can see here. She starts to eat and then a few minutes later she starts to convulse. She gets up panicking and falls into the table. The glass cuts her wrists, and she bleeds out. I'm not saying your outcome was wrong Ellis, I just prefer to have more than one scenario."

Ellis smiles. "No, you're good, and I agree… If we have more than one outcome, we can determine all the possibilities of each scenario and hopefully one of them is the truth. So far, we've gotten two possible outcomes; either the victim had an argument of some sort and was pushed or fell onto the table. Or she was poisoned and fell onto the table. Does anyone else have a theory?"

Westwood stares. "It could be accidental, look here, our Jane Doe has a broken heel. She could have stumbled, broken her heel, and fallen onto the glass table. I mean I know I'm kind of clumsy in heels; I fell a few times. But I… I actually wanted to go back for a second and add something to the who. I think our Jane Doe a high-class type."

"What makes you think she's high-class Westwood, I mean yes at first glance I can tell you her outfit looks expensive, but this is a restaurant, maybe she was meeting someone."

"True Ellis, but I was referring to her shoes. One thing I learned when I was undercover, always pay attention to a person's shoes. Now yes that doesn't really define a person, but to some people the shoes he or she wears can tell you a lot about them, in my opinion at least. Our Jane Doe is wearing top notch high heels. I can tell just by looking at them she must have spent over seven hundred dollars for them at least."

Lowell smiles. "What's with women and shoes? I never understood that. Whenever my wife and I go out, it may take me not even fifteen minutes to get ready. But for some unknown reason she takes hours to get ready and that's just doing her hair and makeup! She takes another hour or so just to pick out her shoes…I mean is it just me?"

Cross laughs. "You said it yourself, it's just one of those unknowns that only women understand. No offense, that's a compliment by the way ladies."

Westwood smiles. "It better be. But yeah, you're right Ellis, a woman's shoes do say a lot about her. I should have caught that and now that you mention it, look at her outfit. I can tell you now with what she has on including her jewelry, she's wearing close to four to five thousand dollars worth. If she was meeting someone, it would have been one hell of a first expression."

Lowell smiles. "I agree and disagree on that. Most men don't usually care about how much a woman's outfit is. Especially if this was just a first date or something. If she was meeting a man, her outfit would be the last thing on a man's mind. I do believe I speak for most men when I say we really don't care how much your outfit cost if we're on a date. So, I believe our Jane Doe was meeting a woman, but that's just my opinion. As far as our what, I'm going with Cross, I think she was poisoned."

Ellis nods. "Ok, Cross and Lowell are saying she was poisoned. I'm thinking argument gone wrong and she was pushed onto the table, and Westwood thinks it could be accidental, her heel broke she stumbles and falls onto the table. All that leaves is you. What do you think Channing?"

Channing sighs, "To be honest, I'm thinking all of you are right."

Everyone stares.

"Not to sound conceited or anything, but just hear me out. Jane Doe here sits at the table and orders her food as we see here, there's food all over the ground after the table shattered. I agree with Lowell when he said he believe she was meeting a woman, why you may ask, because there are two wine glasses on the floor here."

Westwood sighs. "Damn again I should have noticed that, but you're right, if she was meeting a woman, then the preferred drink would be wine. We'll we now know she meant a woman and they had dinner or either she was waiting on our mystery woman, either or…continue Channing."

"Alright, I believe at some point during dinner our Jane Doe was poisoned. By who, we still don't know just yet, it could have been our mystery woman or someone else. But for now, our prime suspect is our mystery woman because obviously if she was poisoned too, we would have two bodies here instead of one."

Ellis smiles. "Obviously… I see you're giving us every detail Channing and that's good and all, but we are on a time limit here. I'm not rushing you, but can you just…

Channing smiles. "Right, sorry, I'm getting there. While enjoying her meal, Jane Doe starts to convulse, and our mystery woman jumps up and puts on an act by trying to help her. In the mist of trying to help her, she gently pushes or shoves our Jane Doe resulting in her broken heel, she stumbles and falls onto the glass table. Now if this was a real restaurant, everyone around would see our mystery woman trying to help our Jane Doe and they would rule it an accident by perception."

Lowell stares. "I see, actually you make a good point, but we still can't say she was poisoned or even if she was poisoned at all."

Channing smiles. "Actually, I think we can, look here at the two wine glasses on the floor. You see what I see?"

Westwood smiles. "Yeah, this one I actually caught. Only one of the glasses is empty, the other is spilled all over the place. So, you think the empty one was the one she drank, and our mystery woman laced it on the count her glass is still full."

Channing snaps his fingers. "Something like that, but again it's just a theory."

Ellis smiles. "Yes, but for now it's the theory we're going with, if we all agree."

Rakes smiles. "We'll look at them go almost brings back memories. Don't you think so partner?"

Gamble sucks his teeth. "I wouldn't say that, we didn't take nearly this long. They already missed a big part of their who, I mean damn how did they miss it and then I even asked if they were done with their who. And in case you've forgotten Rakes, their success is based on our supervision. And what I'm seeing now is their showing we suck at supervising. And I be damn if these rookies mess up my chases of getting promoted, so If I have to sneak a clue in then so be it."

Monroe sighs. "Yeah, I know Gamble; Westwood was on the right track when she noticed Jane Doe was high-class based on what she had on. Lowell too when he mentions she was having a meeting. That right there should have been obvious enough. I mean didn't it occur to them to check the damn reservation list? A simple glance and they would have figured out who was there. It is a little irritating, but even though we're supervising and we can't interfere. Hopefully one of them will figure it out."

Keys smiles. "I think we might need to get you another coffee partner. You seem to be still on edge, we all make mistakes, this is their first time and besides…I like them."

Gamble grunt. "Of course you say that, Keys. Channing is your spitting image."

Rakes whispers to Monroe. "I thought I was crazy you notice that too."

Monroe smiles. "Of course…we got another one."

Rakes smiles. "You're right. It's going to be a long day. Alright, if you're done with your 'what' then let's move on! You got your 'who' and 'what' and again these decisions are yours as a group, so now let's keep it going your halfway there… where and when! I think those two are self-explanatory… and remember your decisions are not just your own but has a group."

Ellis sighs. "Ok, let's start with the 'where'. I guess that's obvious… we're at a restaurant, a very nice restaurant."

Cross stares. "Not just a restaurant, but a restaurant on a docked ship. It's more than just very nice, it's expensive. Looks like our theory of our Jane Doe being high-class is becoming more realistic."

Westwood sighs. "I guess I am really off my game. A place like this will definitely cost an arm and a leg, so now it's clear Jane Doe was a high-class lady who clearly enjoyed the finer things in life."

Lowell smiles. "Don't beat yourself up too much Westwood. Even though Lowell is the best profiler here, we all should have noticed it. Come to think I should have been the first one…I can't believe I forgot."

Westwood stares. "You want to fill us in, the expression on your face is saying its important."

Lowell stares intensely. "Hmmm if I'm not crazy, eight years and seven months ago…it's a bit different, but I'm positive now this is the same restaurant where I propose to my wife."

The group stares.

"Are you sure about that Lowell? This isn't the only fancy restaurant around."

"True Cross, but twelve years ago this restaurant wasn't on a ship. I only just realized it when I actually took a closer look around. Some things aren't what I remember, like I don't remember those chandeliers overhead, and I don't remember this restaurant having a center stage, but this is definitely the same restaurant."

"Well that still doesn't guarantee this is the same restaurant, Lowell. You still haven't told us why you think this is the same one."

Lowell sighs. "You might be right Cross, but I just can't shake this feeling. I don't know, maybe I'm overthinking but let's move on. So, we have our where right…now let's move to our when. Anyone have an idea?"

Channing stares. "Well even though it's fake, the blood is dry. Also, from the feel of it…foods cold. I'm thinking a few hours dead, maybe three or four."

Westwood stares. "I agree, I don't see any sighs of rigger, so she hasn't been dead long. I guess that would be the M. E's determination. Wait a minute what's this… I might be able to make that determinations myself. Ellis, can you do me a favor and tell me the time please?"

Ellis stares with confusion. "Ok… it's twenty pass six."

Westwood smiles. "Look here, looks like her watch stopped. Our Jane Doe was killed at 4:47. Her watch must have broken when she hit the ground."

Ellis smiles. "Good eye Westwood, so now we have our who, what, where and when… so what's next?"

Keys sighs heavily. "I believe Gamble said this earlier. Why do you keep looking at us for validation on what to do next or whether you're right or wrong? Again, as Rakes mentioned before, your decisions and assessments are yours as a group not ours. But if you need us to still hold your hands, then what's next should be the most obvious…Why!? Why did someone want this woman dead? Why now, why today, or if this was an accident why was she taken so abruptly?"

Gamble sucks his teeth. "Always have to be so deep with it, there he goes again."

Ellis sighs. "Well let's break it down then. Once we gather the right information and come to a conclusive determination, our why should answer itself. We have to hurry we are on a time limit, and I do believe our supervisors are getting a little restless."

Westwood smiles. "I don't think restless is the word I would choose. Ok… lets' set the scene. We got our Jane Doe arriving at a restaurant with the intent on meeting someone or maybe that someone was already here before she died. That someone was most likely a woman, we know this because of the two wine glasses on the floor."

Cross smiles. "Right and afterward, we think some point during dinner, our mystery woman slipped something in our Jane Doe glass. Jane Doe starts to convulse, mystery woman pretends to help and pushes Jane Doe into the glass."

Ellis smiles. "After she's pushed or trips, the glass shards cut through her neck and wrists severing her veins and she bleeds out."

Lowell sighs. "I actually have some reservations on that. I mean even if she was pushed or tripped into the glass table, how could our killer woman have known the glass would cut her wrists? I mean people fall through tables and mirrors all the time and yet only a few are deadly. I don't know, maybe the glass cutting into her neck and wrists was an unforeseen incident, but fortunate for our mystery lady."

Westwood sighs. "I actually was thinking the same thing, Lowell. I mean think about it, if I just put some kind of poisoned in your glass then the job is done. The poison is already going to kill you; all that means is that the glass cutting the neck and wrists was an unknown unfortunate. So, does this mean what we're all thinking?"

Channing stares. "Yea…our Jane Doe was already dead before falling into the table. Before you asked, I think we can confirm this because I just noticed something. Honestly, I'm kicking myself because we all should have notice it right away. Look at her wrists more closely…see it now?"

Ellis pauses and sighs. "Your right Channing, looking closely Jane Doe has a single parallel laceration on each of her wrists that are deeper cuts than the others."

Westwood sighs. "Which means our mystery woman, after poisoning her, cut Jane Doe wrists? Why? It seems we know it was intended, but why? Sorry I guess that's what we're supposed to be answering. So, we all agree that she was poisoned, but naturally that's up to the M.E to determine and verify that. I actually don't even know how we are supposed to determine that, after all this is just a simulation. So how are we supposed to verify our determinations?"

Cross smiles and whispers. "Well, I guess we'll cross that bridge in due time. But it seems like we still have a slight problem, our supervisor still looks irritated. It's almost like their saying we missed something, because if not they would have told us the next phase. Am I right…I mean we got everything but our why, so…did we miss something?"

Channing stares. "I agree, so let's look around."

It's amazing isn't it...just from a glace the brain can record and store whatever it is you saw or seen. Past or present rather from 20years ago or two minutes ago, you've may have forgotten but the brain never did forget. The real question would be how does the brain store the right information that one needs through-out life? Is it from a certain trauma? Or a specific trigger from a memory? In my own personal opinion, I would think it's similar to dreams. Think about it... 80percent of the time a person can't remember their dreams...unless it's a specific or reoccurring dream. To me specific and reoccurring is the brain's way of telling you, you might want to remember this. Or better yet you might not want to forget this. Or just maybe it's that 80percent...you wake up... and it's nothing.

"Well Ellis you're known to be the puzzle master. Are you seeing something we missed? I can't say for sure Channing...but now that you mention it, take a closer look at where we are. Can you be a little more specific Ellis; I mean we're at a restaurant."

Ellis smiles. "To be exact, we're at the V.I.P section of said restaurant Cross. I'm still not following you here Ellis, are you going somewhere with this? There is only one thing every fancy restaurant with a V.I.P section has in common... a reservation."

Cross smiles. "And here we are calling her Jane Doe and it didn't occur to any of us to check the damn reservation list. Yeah, if I was our supervisor, I guess I would be irritated too; I wouldn't be surprised if we've already failed. Yea, your right Cross and not to mention our failure is their failure. So, we need to get our act together and show them we can do this."

Westwood stares. "I can tell something is on your mind when you start to zone out. What's bothering you, Lowell?"

Lowell smiles. "You profiling me Westwood? Of course, you are it's in your nature. Don't worry, that was meant to be a compliment. Well in this case you'd be right, out of all the restaurants in this city why choose this one as our crime scene? That's right you mention you purposed here Lowell. I guess it is a little strange, but I don't think it's related, maybe a little consequential."

Channing stares. "Maybe not…Lowell I think you're right, here take a look at this reservation list."

Lowell stares intensely. "What the hell is this? That's… what's my name doing on this list!? Is this part of this stupid simulation!? If it is it's going too far, talk about personal, how the hell did they know where I propose to my wife. Come to think, hey Westwood what time did you say Jane Doe was killed? I believe you said 4:47. Well hell I guess old age is starting to take its toll on my memories. If I'm not mistaken, I booked the reservation for 4:00 and proposed almost an hour later."

Westwood stares. "So not only is this the same restaurant you took your wife to. You're saying that your proposal and our Jane Doe murder happen almost at the same time? No, I don't think that was consequential, it was planned. I don't know if this is part of the simulation, but don't over react too much Lowell, were still being watched. That's easier said than done Westwood, but you don't seem to understand what I mean. I only recently told you four about where I proposed, so I ask again how the hell did they know? Think for a minute, and maybe I'm over reacting a little, but knowing the exact restaurant and time a person's proposed? I mean that's not actually something a person can look up on the internet."

Ellis sighs. "Yeah, you're right that is weird, do you think they knew about this? I don't know Ellis, maybe this is a test or something. Look at them they're just standing there staring, I wouldn't put it pass it if they did know something about this…especially that Detective Keys."

Channing stares. "Before we get ahead of ourselves and start pointing fingers, let's get back on track. Everyone spread out and keep searching. And what exactly are we searching for Channing? I don't know yet Lowell if I'm guessing, then its' something that we all missed."

Westwood sighs. "I don't know Ellis, I almost didn't want to say anything, but I have to say I kind of agree with Lowell. It is kind of eerie that someone knew where and when Lowell proposed. I mean he has a point, unless you were here 8 years ago, how could you have known?"

Ellis sighs. "Yeah, actually I've been thinking the same thing, but I didn't want to over think things. Well like our fearless leader Channing said, before we get ahead of ourselves let's keep looking around and get this over with."

Westwood side smiles. "You got that too…and I thought it was just me. It's crazy and a little disturbing on how much they put into a simulation. I know it's supposed to be a little real so we can get the actual experience, but c'mon. These mannequins almost look like your normal people at a restaurant. Everyone is eating and looking like their having just your normal everyday conversations."

Lowell scoffs. "I'm leaning more to disturbing then crazy Cross. I'll be glad when this stupid simulation or whatever the hell it is to be over with."

Cross sighs heavily. "Are you still on that Lowell? C'mon yes, it is a little disturbing, but I'm sure it was just part of this simulation. After all they did say they wanted to make this as real as possible. I have to admit though, all this does look real to me."

Cross chuckles. "Hey look at this one, everyone around here is eating their food, but he has a table by himself and… is he reading the newspaper? Who the hell reads the newspaper at a restaurant? I thought the only places to read the newspaper were at coffee houses or your bathroom?"

Ellis smiles. "Men… I see nothing wrong with reading the newspaper. Doesn't matter where you are, I happen to enjoy a good newspaper when I'm at a restaurant myself. Really Ellis? Well, I'm not reading it actually Cross, I play the crosswords they have. Why is that a problem for you?"

Cross smiles. "Not a problem at all, as a matter of fact, it would seem you and this mannequin have that in common. What are you talking about Cross? Have what in common?"

Ellis stares with shock. "…Oh shit…? Hey! You can dock points for asking questions later, but I need to know what the hell is this!?"

Gamble grunts. "Looks like the shy one got some bass in her voice. I'm starting to like her. This is taking too long, I was starting to fall asleep. What's the problem here?"

Ellis scoffs. "I mean no disrespect, but simulation or not something like this is too personal. Someone needs to explain now, or I walk… sir.

"Explain what exactly Ellis? Oh, I know, how about the fact that you five are already on the fast track at failing here. Can you explain that? Or how about we've been here for almost two hours, and you still haven't even figured out your 'who' yet. Can you explain that? You want to talk about personal. You see we're personally responsible for your success here, which to be blunt, you fail we fail. And as I mentioned before, you're about thirty minutes away from completely failing here without even needing the six hours. Can you explain that? No…of course not…so now that we're in this little time out here, what's got you so edgy?"

Ellis sighs. "I'm sorry sir, but I need to know how you got this, and where did you get it from?"

Gamble scoffs. "You're looking at me like I'm supposed to know what you're talking about."

Keys sighs. "She's not looking at you Gamble; she's looking at me. Something on your mind Ellis?"

Ellis stares intensely. "Again, I mean no disrespect, but is all this your doing? Up to this point, we've all chalked these incidents up as consequential. I now know if anything but… with that in mind, what I need for you to explain is this." Ellis slams the paper on table. "And before anyone say anything, this is not just a normal crossword puzzle… it's my crossword puzzle."

"I'm still not seeing the issue here Ellis. You're getting all bent out of shape because a mannequin is holding a puzzle? I suppose even if it is yours that is a little weird, but so what?"

"Easy partner, Ellis here is clearly upset so we need to give her a chance to explain."

Gamble scoffs. "We don't have time for this Rakes and speaking of, did you forget this has a time limit?"

"No, I didn't forget, but you were the one who called the time out, so give her a chance to explain."

Monroe sighs. "She's right Gamble, you put your foot in your own mouth, and besides, we're wasting even more time listening to you complain. Now don't misunderstand me Ellis, Gamble might need some more training in manners, but he's not wrong on some points. This whole simulation is taking way too long and if it wasn't for my suspicions I would have fallen asleep a long time ago. But before I get into that, since we're in this little time out of ours, why don't you tell us about this crossword puzzle?"

Ellis sighs. "As I told him ma'am, it's not just a crossword puzzle; it's my puzzle. To be more specific, it's the same puzzle I was doing last month."

Everyone stares.

"I know what you're all thinking and yes, I'm 100% sure this is mine."

"What makes you so sure Ellis?"

"Because growing up there were two things that I was intently passionate about. The first was being a detective and the second was completing every crossword puzzle that I could do. One of my goals is to enter the world's crossword tournament. To some the second thing might be a little weird, but I have my reasons."

Keys smiles. "Not weird at all. I can understand that, but you still haven't told us how you know this particular crossword is yours."

Ellis blushes. "Again, it might be a little weird, but each time I start a crossword I draw seven circles in the top left corner… a sort of a caterpillar doodle if you will. Whenever I finish a puzzle, I draw a butterfly in the top right corner… a sort of accomplishment that I completed a difficult puzzle, it's just a thing I do."

Gamble grunts. "Yeah, a dumb thing, but you're right about one thing, you're definitely weird. Don't worry about it, an annoying thing that some people do, yeah, we know all about that. Well, I'll be damned. Look here Monroe, seven circles, just like she said."

Monroe stares. "There's no butterfly or rather, there's only half a butterfly and why are five of these circles crossed out?"

"That's the problem, ma'am. On a personal note about myself, I'm a little OCD. Once I start something, I have to finish it, no matter how long it takes. This particular puzzle has taken me over six months to finish and call it pride, but I don't like anything beating me."

Keys grins. "And what makes this particular puzzle so difficult?"

Ellis stares. "Because this puzzle's questions are in the form of riddles. There are only fourteen questions, and I completed all but three. The riddle I was currently on; I wasn't able to solve it…yet."

Monroe sighs. "Well, that explains why five of the seven circles were crossed out. I guess now I can see why you were upset, being so close to finish something and can't finish would be irritating."

Cross chuckles. "Oh yeah, I think I've heard of those puzzles. So, tell us Ellis, what was the riddle?

"What's the point in telling you, Cross? It's not important."

Monroe smiles. "Well, I don't know about that Ellis. It might be my partner rubbing off on me, but you never know what might be important. After all, who besides Gamble doesn't like riddles? So, what was the riddle?"

Ellis sighs. "I'll tell you only on one condition… that if any of you know the answer, please don't tell me. The riddle is: 'I am the key to failure; I am the key to victory. I'm the key to everything, and yes that includes history. All humans use me and even animals too. I can kill and I can save so be careful, how you use me…well that's up to you'."

Gamble laughs. "What the hell does that even mean?"

Ellis blushes and scoffs. "Each time I solve a difficult question, I cross out a circle, a sort of achievement for myself. This might be nothing and unimportant to some; but to me, it's everything."

Rakes sighs. "We get it Ellis, and no one here is judging you, well, maybe except Gamble. It is strange that something this important to you would just show up at a fake crime scene. One, why would something like this even be here? And two, who would even put something like this here in the first place? Tell me Monroe, was this one of those suspicions you mention earlier?"

Monroe stares. "Something like that, but we shouldn't get ahead of ourselves you five still have a simulation to get through. Once you've done that, we'll revisit this situation with the sergeant and hopefully get clarification. That goes for you too Lowell, don't think we didn't notice your hesitation when you were reading the reservations list."

Lowell scoffs. "Of course you did. If you notice it, why didn't you say anything?"

Keys sighs. "As she said we only noticed the look on your face. Obviously something had your skin crawling, but we didn't know what. We really noticed when you told the rest of your group and afterward everyone looked at me with that icy stare that you're giving me now. So let me guess, whatever you saw or figured out, you must have figured I had something to do with it. Am I right?"

Channing sighs. "Yes sir, there's no denying that for a few moments in that time we did suspect you. But I think we all just got a little carried away on account of what we found. Lowell should be the one who tells you on the count it is about him."

Lowell sighs. "It may or may not be related to Ellis' situation, but it's starting to look that way. Not to bore you with the details, but I'm pretty sure this restaurant was the same one I propose to my wife."

Rakes gasps. "Well, that's something…you said pretty sure, what makes you sure Lowell?"

"Well, we had the same thought, but then Channing showed me the reservation list and there it was. My name was on that list, and yes, it's mine because that's my own signature. You might be thinking it was forged but I can assure you it's the same one. I know this because I messed up writing it because I was nervous."

Keys stares. "I see, but I'm still not seeing the accusations towards me. Even with history like mine, do you honestly see me doing something like this? I mean if there were like eight dead bodies around then you know, I could see that. But setting something like this takes time…a lot of time."

Channing stares. "Something like what sir. Don't worry Channing, he's just doing his thing. But we're getting off topic again. Not saying that what Lowell and Ellis discovered was unimportant, but as I said before, let's finish this simulation and then we'll get back to it."

Gamble scoffs. "Well, I do believe I mentioned that earlier Monroe. Now that you agree that we've wasted enough time here, can we un-call this time-out now?"

"For once I agree with you Gamble. Don't get used to it. Now If we're all back on track, then yes, let's get back to the scene. Someone want to tell us where we're at?"

Westwood sighs. "We got three out of five of our who, what, where, when, and why. The two that we're still missing is the who and why. But on that same note, before we got sidetracked, we were just about to figure out our 'who'. Sorry Lowell, but if you could ignore the whole your signature thing, can you tell us our Jane Doe's name?"

Lowell scoffs. "According to this V.I.P reservation list, there was one section reserved for 4 pm today. These sections are divided by color: blue, red, green, and yellow."

"Humph that's right, I proposed in the red room because it was my wife favorite color."

Cross stares. "Well look at that, can't believe we didn't notice… Look up… the chandelier's light bulbs are different colors. That's right Lowell, you mentioned that this restaurant didn't have chandeliers before. Guess it's all coming back to you. Let's see here, well if my eyes are correct, looks like our Jane Doe is under the yellow one. Wow… now someone want to tell me how the hell we missed that? And furthermore, what's the deal with the color code arrangements?"

Westwood grunts angrily. "Good question Cross, not to mention it was right in our faces when Lowell first mentioned it and we still missed it. Sloppy… very sloppy. We should have noticed something so obvious. Damn… doesn't matter now, so let's get along with it. Lowell, she was in the yellow section; what name was reserved for this section?"

(Ship's horn blows)

"What the hell was that!? Did that come from the ship?"

Ellis stares. "Did you say something Westwood? Man, that was loud, I can barely hear anything out my left ear. Does that mean our time is up or something? The sergeant did say we're on a time limit."

Gamble scoffs. "As much as I wish that were true and want this to be over with, I don't think that's the case. Sgt. Williams did say they would be watching. I'm thinking this is his way to move things along with this simulation."

"You might be right, partner, but his way almost caused myself and Ellis to go deaf."

"Well, if it is his way of telling us to hurry alone then I guess we should take the hint."

(Horns blows again)

"Alright… dammit we get it already! Monroe, you know Sgt. Williams better than we do, is this something he's known for doing?"

"I couldn't really say for sure, Rakes; It's not like we hang out every day. Besides this is the first time, as far as I know, that he has hosted a simulation before. I'm just in the dark as everyone else is. Be that as it may, whether it is the sergeant's doing or not, I do believe we should keep this simulation going."

Ellis sighs. "We've been in this area too long, we already got the gist of what happen to our Jane Doe, so I think we should look around for more clues. I don't know. What do you guys think?"

Cross scoffs. "Look at that, the quiet one finally said something I'm sure we all can agree with. This whole simulation is making me anxious; I honestly just need my cigar."

Westwood sighs. "Well, that's one thing I can agree with you on, Cross. This simulation is starting to creep me out, especially since I've haven't even had my coffee today. I tend to get a little irritated, I can hardly function. So, before that horn blows again, can we get this over with?"

Channing sighs. "Well, there is one thing I'm pretty sure we all can agree on. I'm pretty sure we failed this simulation long before that horn blew. But at least let's see this through, so I also agree with Ellis and let's look around for clues to our Jane Doe murder."

"Well Mr. Fearless Leader, where do you suppose we should start looking for these clues? And on that note, what exactly are we looking for?"

"I'm not too sure about that Cross, just going on our theories. It goes back to our what on what we think killed our Jane Doe. If memory serves, we said she might have been poisoned and the killer made it look accidental. We think while she was convulsing, our killer may have shoved her onto the table. But we also stated that before, or most likely after, she fell that our killer slit her writs. Can we all agree with that scenario?"

Lowell stares. "Actually Channing, you suggested that, and we considered it another possibility. Not trying to be an ass or anything, I just like to be specific. But all and all, your scenario I can say might be the likeliest outcome. So, I'll roll with that theory for now. So, what's the plan, I'm thinking we should split up or something? We can cover more ground."

"Good idea Lowell and plus we mentioned it before, we don't need to waste any more time. I want to start with the kitchen. I want to check out our Jane Doe's food preparations."

Westwood grins. "That's a good start, if she was poisoned, then hopefully we'll find something in the kitchen, I'm going with you Channing."

"Me too, as I said before, I think this theory is the strongest, so I'll go too."

Ellis sighs. "I think I'll check out the restrooms. We know our Jane Doe was with a woman based on the wine glasses. Assuming she was our killer, she would have needed a place to change after supposedly shoving our Jane Doe in the table."

Cross chuckles. "Look at that, she's on a roll today. Another good idea from the quiet one, the restroom would be the first place a person runs to change after an altercation in a public place. In fact, I have to go myself so if you don't mind, I think I'll join you."

Channing grins. "Alright Lowell, Westwood, and I will go check out the kitchen while, Cross, you and Ellis check out the restrooms. Let's work our way around and meet up back here at the dining room area in about half an hour. Hopefully things start to make sense by then."

Rakes smiles. "Well look at them go; they're starting to get the hang of it. Divide and conquer will definitely get things going around here."

Monroe sighs. "Yeah, I agree, so let's follow suit and split up with them. Gamble you and Rakes go with Cross and Ellis… Keys and myself will go with Channing, Lowell, and Westwood. I know we're all ready for this to be over with, so just grin and push through it."

Keys stares at Rakes. "Yeah, I know… and she can handle it."

Did you see it… or did it already hit you in the face? If you've been with me so far then you know what I'm talking about. The multiple curveballs of Fate. It's one of life's categories of… it just is what it is, no logic, no science, it's just always there. Example: there is one factor in life that no human or animal can ever determine or predict… the unknown. Whatever a person does in life, whatever a person planned to do in life, or whatever that particular goal is in life, there is always that unknown that can never be anticipated. Now that notion can of course be positive or negative, but in a situation like this or similar situations, it's always the latter. The reason being, when dealing with the multiple balls of Fate, to me it's sort of similar to a magic trick. If

you pay too much attention to the magician's hand, then you've already missed the trick.

Monroe stares sternly. "That's twice you said that, don't think I didn't hear you before. She can handle it… what exactly can I handle?"

Keys side stares. "That's a good question you need to ask yourself Monroe. Two weeks… no call, no text, no letter in a bottle, this the first we've spoken since this morning. Now don't get me wrong, I'm not asking you to pour your heart out or anything. It's your business, but we've been partners for a while I would be lying if I said I wasn't concerned. Clear as day that when I first saw you, after ignoring me that something was on your mind, but you know me I'm not the prying type. If you want to bottle up whatever it is you got going on, then like I said before you can handle it. But if you got something to say, then say it."

Monroe sighs with concern. "Now is not the time, ask me again after this is over."

Westwood stares shockingly. "Wow, this kitchen is nothing less than five stars. Guess that would make sense for this type of restaurant."

Lowell scoffs. "Yeah, and if memory recalls, the meal we had cost more than my car note. Alright, what are we looking for again? Our Jane Doe's last meal, right?"

Channing nods. "Yes sir, but can anyone remember what she had? I can't really recall; everything was scattered across the floor."

"Well on that note, instead of looking for her last meal, shouldn't we be looking for the wine she had? I mean we all believe that if she was poisoned then it was through the wine she drank… right?"

"Yes, you're right Westwood, but we also believe that the killer laced the wine either before or during the time they were at the table. So, the killer couldn't have laced the wine here in the kitchen, too many people would be around."

"But that same scenario would also apply to the food preparation."

Lowell grunts. "So why are we here then, Channing? If both scenarios don't even start in the kitchen, what's the point of being here?"

Channing grins. "That's exactly why where here Lowell… we're going to run the scenario. But before we start, we need to know what she ate. Westwood, do you mind running back and taking a look?"

"Fine, guess it pays to be thorough. Alright, I'll be back."

Lowell stares. "Tell me something Channing. I see the reason in running this scenario to get a gist of what might have happened here. What I don't get is your reason for this."

Channing stares. "First, it was Westwood profiling me, now you too Lowell? If you're asking if I have an ulterior motive or something, then I can assure you I do not. I just like to think outside the box every now and then."

"I wouldn't call it outside the box really Channing, I can't really put my finger on it, but I'll figure it out."

"There's really nothing for you to figure out Lowell but keep at it, I guess."

Westwood pants. "Hey sorry about that, I got a little lost. It took me a while to get back, this place needs a map or something. Anyways, even though the food was all over the place, I got a general idea of our Jane Doe's meal. Looks like she had some type of soup and what looks like a house salad. I didn't see anything else around the table, so I don't believe our mystery woman had anything. That also can confirm that our Jane Doe was first to arrive to the restaurant."

Lowell stares. "Well yes and no, I mean our mystery woman may not have been hungry. You have to ask yourself if you were the killer, would you order a full meal? No, the job of any professional killer is to get in and out without leaving anything behind."

Channing stares. "Actually, you're both sort of right. Our mystery woman could have arrived first and just order Jane Doe's meal. That also can apply to the wine she drank. But that's why we're here to figure it out."

"And run that by me again Channing, just how are we supposed to figure that out. We don't even know when she was poisoned and on that same note, was she even poisoned to begin with? All of this is just circumstance and theories."

"That's true Lowell, but we're not really looking for a when she was poison, at least not right now… more like a how. Let's take a quick run through what we know. We know that our mystery woman didn't poison the wine or food here in the kitchen on the count there were too many cooks around."

Westwood nods and smiles. "We can also rule out her having spiked the wine while they were sitting at the table. I don't really see our Jane Doe being that clueless and also, we've established that she was a high-class woman. Most people don't realize, but high-class people are very detailed in the food and drinks they order. Trust me, when her food and drinks arrived at the table, I guarantee our Jane Doe checked her order to make sure it was just right."

Lowell chuckles. "Actually, I can say I agree with that, sounds just like my wife. Now my wife is not like this type of high-class woman, but any time she orders any type of meal, especially at a drive through, believe you me she will check it at least three times. But back to what we were talking about, you're right Westwood, I really don't see out killer being that bold. Even if this was a professional, which I'm highly considering, I don't see her doing that."

Channing stares. "Highly considering? So, you think she was targeted? Yes sir, I do Channing, think about it for a moment and look how she was killed. If we're still holding on to our theory, Jane Doe was poisoned then her wrists were slit most likely after she was pushed in the table. The point is all this was premeditated and well thought out."

Channing smiles. "You're right Lowell and that notion right there is why we're here. How could our killer plan something like this in a crowded restaurant?"

"To my knowledge, there are only two ways that could happen. In all my years as a former soldier, it was the planning that took the longest. It would take weeks if not months to study a target. One way that this could happen is that our mystery woman knew our Jane Doe. We did establish that Jane Doe did meet our mystery woman, but for what reason is still unknown. The second way this could happen is what you said Lowell. I'm thinking she was targeted, and our mystery woman took the first window she had and slipped the poison. The only thing that bothers me is that if it is the ladder rather than the former, then how can you already plan a kill in a crowded restaurant? There would be too many unknown varieties to account for."

Westwood smiles. "I can see your point Channing, but don't get ahead of us just yet. How about we start on the how part as you suggested earlier and then hopefully everything else will fall together. Also, I'm starving, haven't eaten all day and being here in this kitchen is not helping my hunger pains."

Lowell side smiles. "I'm with you on that Westwood, even though this is just a simulation they really went all out, look in the window even the food is real. Hmmm looks good whatever it is… smells even better. Let's see, what do we have here? Looks like smothered pork chops with a little grilled mushroom, side of asparagus and what looks like mac and cheese with something red mixed in with it. Also, what's this white stuff supposed to be… mayo or something? That's the thing with some of these high-class dining, they mix food where it doesn't belong. Mayo shouldn't be nowhere near pork chops or anywhere near here for that most. What I'm talking about my wife does the same thing, does sort of looks good though whatever it is?"

Westwood stares with shock and fear. "Their bacon bits Lowell… mac and cheese with bacon bits. And your right mayo doesn't belong on pork chops, but it's not mayo… it's ranch. Detectives I'm sorry for wasting your time and the inconvenience but I'm regretting to say… I quit."

Monroe sighs. "Didn't depict you as a quitter Westwood. Out of the five of you, you were the last one in my mind I thought would quit. However, I am curious to know why you want to quit. You got this look on your face, a look that I haven't seen in a long time."

Keys sighs. "I agree the look she's talking about is well known especially in this line of work. That look on your face Westwood is the look of fear. When you notice that food on the plate it was almost like you saw a ghost."

Westwood angrily sighs. "In a way I guess you can say that. Smothered pork chops with grilled mushrooms. Mac and cheese with bacon bits mixed in it. And a side of asparagus with a cup of ranch, I've always told him you need to eat more vegetables. What are you talking about Westwood, told who? My husband Lowell… I always told him to eat more vegetables… and he would always smile and laugh. Detective Monroe, you were right in saying out of the five of us I would be the last to quit. That's because one of the main reasons I chose to become a cop was because of him. My husband was my other half and supported me every step of the way. I lost my husband five years ago… wrong place wrong time when a robber wanted his car and instead of just taken it, he took the only man I've ever loved."

Monroe sighs. "I'm sorry to hear that and I'm sorry for your loss. But not to sound invasive, you still haven't told us why you want to quit."

"I'm quitting, Detective." Westwood sheds a tear. "Because of that plate of food over there. I know that might be strange to you, but to me it means more than you know. To elaborate on that ghost remark of yours Detective Keys, that plate of food is what my husband orders every year on our anniversary. Our first date that's what he ordered, and I made that crack about eating vegetables. After that every year on our anniversary that was our meal, and we would just laugh. Seeing that plate of food over there is too much for me to bear. Not only is this way too personal, it's heartless and cruel to even considering putting something like this here."

Keys stares. "I agree it is heartless and cruel, which is leading me to believe even more that this isn't part of the simulation. Just now, you Westwood makes three out of the five recruits that discovered something that is personal to you during this whole supposed simulation. Lowell, it seems was first with his marriage proposal, then Ellis and her crossword puzzle obsession, and now you Westwood with the anniversary meal. There is an old saying that still holds true today; one time is consequential, two or more time, it's a pattern."

Monroe side smiles. "For once I'm ahead of you on that Keys, I had the same feeling after Ellis and her crossword ordeal. I don't like it; something is definitely not right with this whole simulation. Westwood, I know you want to quit, but I need you to do me a favor and stay just a bit longer. I hate to ask, but if there is something wrong with this whole simulation then I don't want whoever is behind this to get off track. Trust me, I know how you feel; I was married before, so I know how the little things you share with your husband are the most cherished. But right now, I need you three to pull yourselves together and continue this simulation. (Channing sighs. "They're right, this whole thing is off, but if we start making a scene then we'll never figure out who's behind this. Are you two ok to finish this thing?"

Lowell scoffs. "I've never been the one to start something and not finish. Besides if I walked away the thought of not knowing would eat me alive. How about you Westwood? I get the sense we're similar, I would never hear the end of it from my wife if I walked away no matter the reason. I may not have met your husband before, but seeing how you talk about him I would have imagine he would say the same thing… am I wrong?"

Westwood sniffs and grins. "No, he definitely wouldn't let me live it down and that right there is why I'll continue to go alone with this. I just have one request, if it turns out to be true and someone is behind this, then once we catch him… he's mine."

Keys smiles. "I think we all can agree with that, it's a deal Westwood, but I have only one stipulation for you, once we figure out who he is he's yours, and when I make a deal I keep it, but you can't kill him. So now that we're all in an agreement, why don't you three continue on where you left off, I'll find a way in letting the others know later on."

Westwood sighs. "Good the quicker we finish this thing the better I would be. Hey, Channing, I know you wanted to run this scene of yours to find out when and where our killer could of spike Jane Doe's wine. But can we hold off on that for a minute? I think we should check on Ellis and the other first and see if they found something. Like the detectives told us before our findings are as a group."

Lowell grins. "You beat me to it Westwood I was about to say the same thing and plus we did agree to meet up anyways in half an hour."

Channing smiles. "Yeah, you're right maybe they got something, but before we go let's at least give this kitchen a good work over. We really didn't search the place and I don't want us to miss anything. Yeah, I can't argue that Channing, we did get sidetracked over my drama over that plate of food. So that's on me, alright let's get this done… Maybe Ellis and Cross are doing better than we are."

Ellis sneezes. "Oh great, I've searched this bathroom from top to bottom and not only did I find nothing, now someone is talking about me. I don't know, maybe this was a dumb idea. If this was professional there's no way the killer would leave something behind, let alone in a bathroom."

Rakes grins. "Don't beat yourself up too much Ellis nothing is really a dumb idea when looking for evidence. Plus, I would have suggested looking in the restroom myself if that's any comfort. You said you thought this was professional, I mean you can never be too careful right? Yeah, I guess you're right Detective, it's just my mind isn't all the way here at the moment. Seeing my crossword here still got me on edge, I barely can see straight. I'm always careful with my personal stuff especially my crosswords, so how the hell did it end up here of all places? It's eerie to think, but there's only one way to me that someone could have known about my crosswords. I have no enemies that I know of so that only leaves one outcome… I think I got a stalker. Not to sound conceded, but to know how passionate I am with my crosswords and to know the one I was working on. To know all that and to put it here at a murder simulation, it's just insane it actually goes a little pass stalking. Oh, I'm sorry Detective I'm getting sidetracked again I need to get my head back in the game. All this overthinking it's no wonder I can't find anything. I guess I'll check in with Cross and see if he found something in the men's restroom."

Rakes stares. "I thought your mind was somewhere else Ellis, and on a side note I think you're right about your stalker situation. You will also be right in putting that thought to the side for now and focus. Now this doesn't count as helping, but just asking out of curiosity, are you sure everything looks good here? I mean I don't want to confuse you or anything. If you say everything looks good and you want to check in with Cross then we'll move on, I just want to make sure your mind is back in the game. Sometimes when looking for evidence you have to look for something that is not there or doesn't belong."

Ellis smiles. "You do that too; I always think out loud it helps me focus better. Now that I'm back in the game I guess before checking in with Cross I'll give this place another check, you know just to be sure. Actually, when looking a little closer there is something that stands out in this restroom. It's clean… I mean really clean even for a restroom for this type of restaurant. Hmmm toilets are clean, sinks and mirror are shining, and floors look like you could eat a five-star meal off of. Everything seem to be spotless except… that… the trash is full. A trash can that is full in a nearly spotless restroom is some-thing that stands out. Damn, how the hell did I just notice that. Alright lets' get this over with."

Ellis knocks over can. "Oh man what is that smell? Is that a diaper, you did say they wanted to give us a real experience, but they could have left this out. I hate to think of what the men's trash looks like. Sorry yes, I know De-tective, focus right? I got it. Ok other than the full diaper, what do we have here; gum wrappers, a lot of used paper towels, and an empty bottle of lotion. Hmmm seems to be just gum wrappers and used paper towels, typical of what you would find in a lady's restroom trash can. So am I missing something, the trash was the only thing standing out. What's this, maybe I was looking in the wrong place, there's something stuck to the side of the can. Looks like chewed gum, that's gross by the way, I know not to touch it don't want to contaminate the DNA on it. I know it's a long shot, but this gum could belong to our killer, she might have been trying to steady her nerves or something. No, I take it back, seems too much of a stretch, I mean if this murder was done by a professional then she wouldn't need to steady the old nerves." Ellis whispers to herself, "C'mon Ellis, get it together, obvious Detective Rakes seen something that I missed, so what could it have been? Gum on the side of a trash can is something that doesn't belong, but regrettably it's common. Wait a minute, there's something stuffed in this gum. What the hell is that? Excuse me, Detective, can I barrow a pair of tweezers and a plastic bag?"

Rakes side smiles. "Sure… here you go, so you're going to bag the gum, do you think it's relevant? I mean after all it could belong to anyone number of women who have been in here. Not sure at the moment Detective, but there appears to be something stuck in the gum. After all I'm sure you noticed that, but it's all good. Now let's see what we have here. Looks like some sort of chain, a gold chain to be specific, but its small too small to go around a person's neck. I'm sure this was intended, our killer or someone place this chain in the gum and stuck it to the side of the trash can. The question is why… could it be whoever place this here was trying to hide the chain or was it place here for safe keeping. On that note our Jane Doe could have placed this here as some sort of precaution. Either way something like this definitely doesn't belong here. If I were to have a theory I would say after killing our Jane Doe, our killer took the chain, which I'm assuming belong to Jane Doe, she came to the restroom and stuck the gum and chain to the trash can. I'm also assuming the chain might be worth something or is important somehow to our killer. She stashed it here so as to come back later when everything calmed down. What… was that too much, I was getting ahead of myself wasn't I?"

Rakes smiles. "I didn't say anything Ellis, this is your show I'm just watching. But I will say that is one thing we share, I do actually talk out loud a lot, and Gamble is always telling me to slow down when we are at a scene. Piece of advice and this still doesn't count as helping, but when you have a partner or part of a group, it's good to have your own theories. That way when determining what happened at a scene, everyone's own theory can way in, and you can determine which one is the strongest outcome and go from there."

Ellis smiles. "I appreciate the advice Detective Rakes, so I'll hold on to my theory for now until we'll all meet up. Well now I'm pretty sure that I didn't forget anything in here, so I guess I'll check in on Cross to see if he got anything in the men's restroom."

(Knock Knock)

"Hey Cross, you still in there? I'm coming in."

Cross smiles. "No need for the knock Ellis, I was done a long time ago. Well, I guess I should clarify; I was almost done looking around didn't find anything and I was done using the bathroom. I was actually about to come check in on you, the restrooms here aren't that big, so what took you so long? I take it you must have found something?"

Gamble scoffs, "Think you might want to put some specifics on that clarification, Cross. He took longer using the bathroom than looking around and lucky for me I had to be stuck in here with him."

Rakes chuckles. "Why didn't you just wait outside? It's not like I was in the stall with him Rakes, and then afterward he took five minutes to look around. One hell of a detective this guy is going to make. Well, why didn't you help him Gamble? We aren't supposed to help Rakes…remember."

Cross angrily sighs. "I am still standing right here detectives. And on that earlier note Detective Rakes I asked Detective Gamble not to say a word even if I missed something. In all truth I was going to check and see if Ellis found something. That way I'd have a clearer view of what I was looking for. So, if we could get back to it… Ellis did you find anything in the lady's room?"

Ellis stares. "Actually, I think I may have. I found this stuck to the back of the trash can. It might be something or it might be nothing, but according to some advice I got, it was out of the ordinary. We couldn't figure out… I mean I couldn't out who this belongs to, either our Jane Doe or the killer? I did have a theory, but I was waiting on you to see if you got anything from the men's room. Cross… are you ok… did you hear what I said?"

Cross intensely stares. "Yeah… yeah, I heard you, Ellis. As I said before I didn't really find anything in there, there were no clothes left behind or anything of that assumption. But now that you've found this, I guess we can give the restroom another run through."

Ellis stares. "I know that look, it's the same one I had earlier today… what's wrong Cross? Oh no wait, don't tell me; you know something about this chain, don't you? The way your face turned pale when you saw it, its' the same face I made when I saw my crossword, so this tells me it must hold some significant to you?"

Cross sighs heavily. "That would be an understatement Ellis, but I don't won't to get worked up too quick especially if I'm not entirely sure. Can I see that… well damn…? Hmmm I'm sure you noticed that this chain is too small to go around a person's neck. That's because if I'm right then I think it goes through this. What is that… is that a clock? Yes, to be more specific it's a pocket watch, Ellis. This pocket watch of mine was passed down through my family's generation. Not so much as a family heirloom, but more of a sacred good luck charm. This was given to me by one of my aunts. It was a birthday present when I turned twenty-one. Yes, I know what you're thinking, but there's nothing special about this watch, it's just your everyday plain old pocket watch. It's just very sentimental and it has helped me through the years, I won't knock that. It's precious to my family and I planned on passing it down myself. It's crazy, but now there's no doubt in my mind that this whole simulation is all out of sort."

Gamble scoffs. "I could have told you that from the start Cross. This whole thing is stupid and a waste of time, I mean don't get me wrong I'm not calling you five stupid or anything. I just don't like the idea of being a babysitter."

Rakes sighs. "I don't think that's what he meant partner, but you knew that, you just had to put your two cents into it didn't you? To be frank both Gamble and I noticed the same thing earlier. To be clear the first time it was after Lowell told us about his proposal at this restaurant."

Ellis sighs. "I know you were supposed to be watching us, but if you know something was wrong shouldn't you have told us?"

Gamble chuckles. "Two reasons; one, it's as you said we were just supposed to be watching you five and plus we weren't entirely sure anyways. And two, you were the one who solidified our suspicious Ellis. Your whole crossword tantrum really told us something wasn't right with this whole thing. We didn't want to say anything until we had more concert evident, you know just doing the whole detective thing."

Cross side smiles. "Well to be honest I never thought anything of it, just tossed it up to part of this simulation. But about two years ago I was sitting at this corner café just enjoying the Sunday coffee of the day and all of a sudden there was a small fire from the kitchen. I went to help of course and afterwards the fire department showed up and took care of it."

Gamble angrily sighs. "Did you want a cookie for your heroics or is there a moral here?"

"Sorry Detective Gamble. The moral is before the fire I left my pocket watch on the table and when I came back the chain was missing from the hook. At the time I didn't think much of it, I just thought I dropped it in all the confusions, but now I'm thinking it's all connected somehow."

Ellis stares with shock. "It would appear that tantrum I had earlier wasn't for nothing. That café Cross wouldn't happen to be the Quiet Storm café across from St. Michael's hospital, would it?"

"That would be the one, Ms. Ellis. I take it you know it or saw it on the news?"

"More or less the former, Cross. I should say I know it well on the count I go there one Sunday out of each month."

Rakes side smiles. "Oh, that's right. You did mention something like this before. About how you like doing your crosswords in coffee shops."

Ellis sighs heavily. "Yes ma'am, and after what Cross just said I can't believe I didn't notice it. Honestly, I'm kicking myself for not realizing it sooner. As I mentioned before I go to that café one Sunday out of each month to do my crosswords. It also just so happened I was there that Sunday when that kitchen fire broke out. Coffee of the day I believe was sweet strawberry lattés. I didn't think anything of it at the time because as Cross stated it was just a small kitchen fire, it wasn't that much of a big deal. Thinking back and thinking now, I'm thinking that whole kitchen fire was a set-up. Cross, you mention your chain was missing after the fire was put out. Remember the puzzle I was working on, the same one that mannequin has, that was the same one I was working on. Yes, I know detective Gamble, the moral is when I was walking home, I had this eerie feeling that I was being followed. Turns out I was right because about a month later I was damn sure my home was broken into. There were certain things that weren't in the place I left them in, almost like someone was looking for something. Also, I'll never forget that odor, it was sort of a murky smoky odor almost like burnt cedar."

Rakes sighs. "And let me guess your crossword was stolen? Did you report the break-in to the police?"

Gamble chuckles. "C'mon Rakes, what would she say to the police? 'I want to report a break-in. Someone broke into my house and stole my crossword puzzle.' They wouldn't have taken her seriously, to be honest they would have probably laughed at her. I know I would have."

Rakes side smiles. "Yea, that I can see you doing. So, it would seem our assumptions were right about this whole simulation thing. In fact, I'm starting to think this was a set-up from the beginning. But then that would bring us to one question if that turns out to be true. What question would that be Detective? Well, it's a simple question Cross, if this was a set-up then who was it for? Someone went through a lot of trouble for this. First it was Lowell being in the same restaurant where he proposed. Then you Ellis, finding that mannequin holding your crossword that you just mentioned was stolen from your house. And now speaking of stolen, we have you Cross finding your chain in the restroom, the same chain you said was also stolen. Out of the five of you we discovered three of you that has something in common with this supposed simulation."

Cross sighs. "You mentioned if this was a set-up then who was it for? Just thinking out loud here, but couldn't whoever's doing this be a set-up for you detectives as well? Or maybe even a certain detective."

Gamble grunts. "Would be lying if I wasn't thinking the same thing. But as hard as it is for me to say I don't think this was for this certain detective or any one of us for that matter. I say that with assurance because we aren't the ones encountering anything personal here at this simulation. So far only three of you have something personal here, which leads us to believe if this a set-up of some kind, then it's for one of you five or maybe all of you."

Ellis stares. "Well, we won't know that for sure until we meet back up with the others. But I am with Cross on this I don't want to jump to any conclusions until we are hundred percent sure. To be honest I'm slightly hoping that this whole thinking this was a set-up thing, was just part of this simulation. But when thinking deeper on that notion, I myself am a hundred percent sure this was definitely planned out. Well anyways it's about that time to meet up with the others, so let's get this over with."

Cross grins. "And I thought Channing was pushy. Speaking of that, do you think Channing and Westwood came up with the same conclusion as we did? Besides you, me and Lowell those two are the only ones who don't have any ties to this thing. It's a possibility Cross, but we won't know until we meet up. So, I suggest for the time being that we keep up with this whole simulation charade just to be safe."

Rakes smiles. "She almost reminds me of Keys, look at her she's already trying to think two steps ahead. I guess for the time being we should be trying to do that ourselves, what say you partner? After all I'm sure to notice this by now, but this whole thing… it feels off, but maybe that's me."

Gamble light chuckles. "Now who's thinking like Keys, is this a new thing for you now? Be that as it may I think you're right, but there's another aspect you seem to be overlooking Rakes. If someone is setting this up, who's to say it's not one of them? Now look at me now I'm starting to think like that punk, but I'm sure he would say the same thing. So, let's keep our eyes open and wait and see. After all I'm sure Monroe and Keys are thinking the same thing."

What is fear… no I'm sorry let me ask the right question what is true fear? What is that deep sensation that makes one heart skip a beat and leaves you breathless and frozen? Is it you staring down the barrel of a gun while it's pressed against your temple, just before you hear it cock back? Or how about hearing a deep low growl when walking through the woods on a hike? Or it is just maybe the creaking of a door opening ever so slightly when you find yourself home alone in the dark? When technology fails you and your level of trust in people drops to zero, this

is when true fear creeps in and revels itself. Your muscles get tighter and tighter. The world around you seems to slow down to where the only thing you can hear is your own heart beating faster and faster. Fear often goes by many sayings; fight or flight, it's either you or me, kill or be killed. In any one of these situations there is only one thing that can conquer true fear… ones will to live.

Cross sighs. "Don't need to be a profiler to notice the aggression and tension in the air. I take it you three must have found something in the kitchen that struck a nerve? No need to beat around the bush, I'm sure you already realized it's the same with us. Well, this is a group thing, so who wants to go first?"

Westwood smiles and sighs. "I guess you're right Cross, there is really no need to beat around the bush anymore. Not that we're keeping secrets from each other, but there's no reason to be cautious anymore. I'm sure by now we have all come to the conclusion that whatever this is, it has something to do with one of us. And on that note to answer your earlier statement, that would be me. Channing, Lowell, and I were combing through the kitchen looking for whatever could have killed our Jane Doe. Of course, we agreed it was some kind of poison, most likely in the wine we thinking she drunk. Channing had the idea of trying to recreated the scene on how and when our killer poisoned Jane Doe, but as you can image, we didn't get that far. Before we could do the recreations, Lowell noticed a plate of food on the kitchen counter. I won't go too much into detail, but to sum it up that plate of food was my husband's dish that he ate every year on our anniversary."

Cross stares. "Well, you got me beat Westwood. I can only image seeing something like that, I know for a fact that will definitely strike a nerve. You said it was your husband's dish, the same dish that he has every year for you guy's anniversary, I take it he's…? Yes, Cross, he was taken from me by a car robbery, actually next week would have been our anniversary. So, you can imagine how I felt when I saw that meal, but on that note now it's your turn, what did you find in the restrooms? And before you ask, I'm asking you in particular Cross. It was just you and Ellis, and we all know about Ellis and the whole crosswords situation… so?"

Cross stares. "Astute as ever Westwood, I can definitely see that nerve of yours is certainly struck, as it should be. Well while searching the men's restroom for any kind of clue I didn't find anything, but it was Ellis that did find something… Ellis. In case you're wondering what Ellis is holding in that bag, it a chain, and what does that chain go to you may ask?"

Gamble angrily grunts. "For the love of Pete will you just get on with it already! The chain goes to his pocket watch, the same one he has in his pocket. Sorry Detective Gamble I forgot just trying to build the suspense and technically it's my family's pocket watch that was pass down to me."

Lowell sighs. "If this chain of yours was a family heirloom of a sorts, then how do you supposed it got here? What I mean did you lose it or something or you just now notice it was missing from your watch when Ellis found it? Well, I guess you can say I lost it or something Lowell, Ellis and I were actually trying to figure that out. I won't go too much into detail for Detective Gamble, but we believe my chain was stolen. About two years ago I was at a café when a fire broke out not too long after the fire was put out, my chain was missing. Ellis and I was thinking that fire may have been purposely started."

Channing stares. "What makes you think that? Well, we weren't sure as first, but Ellis shared some facts that made us reconsider."

Ellis grins. "Come to find out I was in that café as well when that fire broke out, but the only thing nothing of mine was stolen. Well, I should say nothing at that moment was stolen, about a month after said fire my house was broken into to… you want to guess what was stolen?"

Channing sighs. "It's starting to make sense, that temper tantrum of yours earlier… so I take it that crossword puzzle was the same one that was stolen from your house? You would be correct sir and you would also be correct in justifying my temper tantrum as you called it. I guess now you can see why I had that little performance."

Monroe sighs heavily. "Alright I think now we all got the gist of everything here. Be that as it may, I still don't want anyone getting ahead of themselves. Yes, I know emotions are high and you all want answers, but if you start to let your emotions get the better of you then that's when you start making mistakes. One thing you five need to know if you're to become detectives is that it's usually the little mistakes that are missed, they are the ones that determine the outcome of a case. As I mentioned earlier, I want you five to continue working on this simulation as if it were just another case."

Westwood angrily sighs. "You're kidding me right!? No disrespect Detective Monroe, but I don't think I can do that. You saw what was in that kitchen didn't you? They have my dead husband's meal sitting right there on the damn counter! You said you can relate to me, so you need to ask yourself could you just ignore everything and continue working as if it were just another case!?"

Keys stares, "I understand your frustration Westwood, but I think you're missing what Detective Monroe is saying. As with everyone here you want answers, right? Well even though you five are still new to this whole detective thing, I'm sure you're starting to realize how it actually is when you got to get your hands dirty. What that means is clearly someone went out their way in setting all this up and the only way in finding who it was is to solve the crime. Or in your case, solve this simulated crime. So, if you five want the answers you deserve you need to keep going with this simulation."

Ellis sighs. "Westwood It's hard for me to say, but I actually agree with them. Don't forget you're not the only one that's been affected here. We all want answers and frustrating as it is the only way we get those answers is to see this thing through. Hey if you're really that angry, why don't you put that into finding out who's behind this. After all I'm sure you got some choice words for him. You're right Ellis, I actually do want to see this through, because I was actually promise something by a certain someone. So, on that note I can guarantee when we do find him there will be no words to be spoken."

Cross stares. "Well, someone is a little dark, but I can understand so no complaining over here. It looks like the ladies are in it till the end as goes for me. What about you two… Lowell, Channing you in? Actually, sorry I guess I should be only asking you that question Lowell. I'm sure Channing is in, after all he's the only one with nothing tied to this whole simulation deal."

Lowell chuckles. "Weren't you paying attention to what Detective Monroe just said about letting our emotions get ahead of ourselves. We still have a case to solve so you never know what we'll find, but to answer your question yes, I'm in I don't think my wife would have it any other way. Channing…?"

Channing grins. "Well despite what Cross or anyone else think whatever is going on here I can assure you it has nothing to do with me. Believe what you want, but I want to see this through just as badly as everyone else."

Lowell smiles. "Well now that's settle what's our next play? If we're still going along with this, then if memory serves, we still don't have a precise idea of what killed our Jane Doe. All we have are theories, but other than our situations we have nothing on our Jane Doe."

Westwood stares. "Well, we might have something. Before my little episode regarding my husband's meal, Channing, Lowell and I were going to do a simulation of our own. If it goes right, we should be able to determine the how and when Jane Doe was supposedly poisoned."

Cross scoffs. "You want to run a simulation to solve a simulation… humph now that's some irony for you. Well, what do you suppose be our next step then Cross? Well since you asked little lady, I propose we split up again. So far, we only search the restrooms and kitchen, this is after all a pretty big ship."

Ellis stares. "That's actually a pretty good idea, but where else to look?" *(Ship's horn blows.)*

"Again, with the horn, that's what, the third time that's happened!?"

"Yeah, and I'm not sure if that was a hint or the answer to your question Ellis. But I'm going to go with the ladder and say I think we should check out the captain's deck."

Lowell looks around. "Don't you think that's a little on the nose Westwood? We were told in the beginning that no one would help us during this simulation. But now, as you stated that's the third time that horn blew, I don't think now someone would be helping us by leading us to our next site."

Channing sighs. "I agree it seems a little too easy don't you think? But then again you might be right Westwood it might be something. And Cross, you did mention you wanted to keep looking around, so I guess we can agree to head to the captain's deck. I don't know if Channing got a bad feeling about that.

Ellis sighs. "I have to agree with Lowell, I don't like it. But to solve this argument we can do what Cross suggested and split up again. Channing you and Westwood can go to the captain's deck and how about we three go back to the dining area and go comb through it again? If we're trying to get back on track with our Jane Doe mystery, then going from the beginning should be a good refresher."

Monroe stares. "I know that look all too well and I think I'm starting to appreciate that thing you do Keys. I take it you already thinking up a plan for this little unfortunate situation? Or rather I should say you must already have several theories and you're trying to determine which is the strongest? As annoying as it is I'm doing the same thing."

Rakes giggles. "Gamble and I mentioned the same thing earlier about how Keys is starting rub off on us. Case in point, she's right Keys just like you we figure this was all kinds of off even from the beginning, but by whom was the question. But I get the feeling as well that you must have saw or seen something, so you mind sharing?"

Gamble grunts. "I wouldn't hold my breath on that Rakes. You should know by now Keys plays everything close to the vest. Which is why I'm sure he's not thinking up a plan, rather I'm sure he already has one or two in motion somewhere. I just wish he would hurry it up, if you wait too long then whoever is behind this just might get to the person thereafter. Imagine how that would reflect on us, supervising detectives played by a rookie cadet or cadets. And here I thought this was supposed to be a normal recertification. But it looks like it turns out that one or more of them is trying to make a statement."

Monroe grins. "When has anything been normal for us Gamble, but you do have a point. This whole thing took time and patience and is well thought out, creepily impressive. Be that as it may I got a bad feeling were getting to the climax. And we're not going to let that happen, so as of now this is no longer a recertification for us, this is now a case that we need to solve before someone gets hurt, or worse. Rakes I want you and Gamble to stay here with Lowell, Ellis and Cross, and Keys and I will go with Channing and Westwood to the captain's deck. I'm sure this doesn't need to be said but be careful. Someone here took great time in planning this and I'm sure he or she doesn't want certain detectives getting in the way, meaning us."

Keys sighs heavily. "Couldn't agree more partner, but I think that ship has sailed a while ago. He finally speaks, and what may I ask is that supposed to mean? Well because Mr. Gamble the ship is actually sailing… this one to be precise."

Rakes gasps. "What are you kidding me Hank, I think we would have realized if this ship was moving. Actually, no we wouldn't have Rakes a ship this size would have motion stabilizers so you wouldn't feel a thing."

Rakes stares with confusion. "So, if we can't feel anything, how can you, and what makes you so sure the ship is even moving? There are no windows in here and none of us have been outside since this thing started. Was it the horn that tip you off, they do blow it before taking off, but even then, that doesn't mean the ship is moving?"

Keys side smiles. "Look up Rakes, notice those chandeliers swaying back and forth? The only thing that can make that happen is when the ship starts to hit waves. The tables, chairs, and mannequins have been bolted down to the ground. So now we're most likely in the middle of the ocean, so your earlier statement about us getting in the way, I don't think that's going to be a problem. To clarify and be brutally honest I'm starting to think none of us going to leave this ship."

Lowell stares. "Humph, wondering what they are whispering about? Alright let's get this over with, Westwood and you and Channing head to the captain's deck. The rest of us will be here in the dining area going through it again. As a matter of fact, something is telling me to take another look at that reservation list."

Ellis sighs. "Well then, I guess Cross and I will take another look at the body and see if we missed something. On second thought I think I'll take another look at that mannequin with my crossword. If I'm not mistaken, I think we're thinking the same thing, Lowell."

All ships lights go out.

"What the hell! What happened? Hey is everyone good, everyone ok!? What kind of question is that Lowell, it's so dark I can't even see my own hand in front of my face. Damn! I don't like this, this doesn't feel right. What the hell happened to the lights? Ellis, Westwood you good, someone talk to me?"

Ellis and Westwood gasps. "Yeah, we're good, but I sure wish I had my gun or something with me. I've been in situations like this once or twice before and it pays to be armed. This is bad, you see shit like this in movies and it always turn out bad when the lights come on."

Monroe yells. "Ok everyone calm down, what we're not going to do is panic! What I need everyone to do is follow the sound of my voice. We need to gather around; we don't need everyone here to be scurrying around the dark."

Keys whispers. "I think that was the point partner, turning off the lights so no one can see you moving around. But telling everyone to gathering around is a good move, just keep your guard. The one in charge is usually the first one targeted."

Rakes gasps, "That's an understatement… I actually got a confession, I really don't do the dark. Especially when the dark follows with this dead silence chill. Oh no please don't say it."

Gamble softly chuckles. "It's quiet… too quiet. You still got that phobia Rakes and how old are you again? But I will half agree with you, being this dead silence, you think you only see it in movies."

Monroe grunts, "Unfortunately, this is no movie, this is real so get serious you two and be quiet. That goes for everyone, come to think everybody just freeze, and be quiet and hopefully the lights will come back on soon." Monroe thinks to herself, 'This is bad I got a bad feeling. Damn I should have acted earlier; I knew this whole thing was wrong from the jump. I let my own personal situation cloud my judgement, if anyone here gets hurt or worse killed, I'll have no one to blame but myself.'

(A door slightly creaks open.)

"Everyone gather closer and stay still. As of this moment I'm calling this off. This is no longer a simulation… this is real."

(Lights come back on)

"Okay no one move… just wait!"

Keys stares and sighs. "Detective Monroe is right we don't need everyone walking around just yet. The good news is that we're all still here, and I want to keep it that way. But on that note, I need you five to do me a favor, just stand still for a few minute and take a good look around the room. Is anything out of sort anywhere, as far as anyone can remember, do anything look out of place?"

Cross scoffs. "No offense Detective, but this whole room is filled with mannequins, from the start this whole thing was out of place."

Channing sighs. "Even though you're right about that Cross, this whole thing is out of place, but Detective Keys is talking about that creaking door we all heard opening. There thinking what we're all thinking, someone was just here. There's only one question that needs to be answered."

Westwood grunts. "Technically there are two questions that need to be answered Channing. Someone was just here there's no denying that, but first question is the obvious, who was is? The second question is a little more difficult. Out of the nine people here are we saying there was someone else here or was it one of us? Not trying to cause any conflicts or hardships, but I know we all thought about it."

Ellis sighs. "Actually, I was thinking the same thing. C'mon guy you can't stand there and tell me that thought having crossed your mind?"

Lowell stares. "Alright even though you're right about that Ellis we don't need to start pointing fingers at each other. For the time being let's just do as the detective says and look around for anything out of place. Humph that's just what I would say if I were the one behind this Lowell. Deflect and turn away from the conversation. Really Cross you want to go there with me, it's funny you're the only one here making a scene! Draw attention to yourself to cause distraction, now what does that sound like to you!?"

Gamble grins. "Still acting like rookies are we!? Well, I guess it can't be helped, but it seems like you five are playing right in whoever is behind this hands. Did you forget what Monroe told you not to do? Pointing fingers at each other is not going to help anyone of us in this situation. Well now this takes me back to one of our first encounters, don't you think? Seems like it's starting to sink in pretty well around here, wouldn't you say partner?"

Rakes side smiles. "Look at you, it's almost look like there are growing on you, but I say that ship sailed long ago no pun attended. I would say it started to sink after Ellis and her whole situation."

Ellis stares with confusion. "Excuse me, but what started to sink in? Can someone tell me what's going on, did we miss something? I thought you said the simulation over Detective Monroe, so if you notice something you can tell us."

Keys sighs heavily. "We did notice something Ellis, but what Gamble and Rakes are talking about, it's not physical, but more so emotional. Honestly you and Lowell started it presuming unknowingly, but still… we're talking about Island fever. It's when you have a group of people trapped in place such as an abandoned house or in our situation a ship in the middle of the ocean. Once the killer realized that you're trapped and helpless, they do the next obvious thing, which is you scare the living shit out of them. Once your victims are good and scared, they literally do the work for you, which is what Gamble meant when he said you're playing right in this person's hand. If you want to be a good detective you can't solve anything with just accusations, and running around pointing fingers, you need evidence to back them up. I know it's frustrating and everyone wants answers, but the only way to get those answers is not to play in the killer's hands. Someone tell me what was the first thing I told you five when you started this simulation?"

Lowell sighs. "Close your eyes and breath… sorry Detective you're right I guess I did get a bit off hinge. This whole thing is not so frustrating, but it's irritating on how whoever is behind this is setting this up. Maybe it's just me, but I almost feel like a rat in a maze being led to the cheese, rather than finding it myself."

Cross stares. "Humph, looks like we have something we can agree on, I actually second that notion. Which is why I'm thinking back on the ship's horn, that horn blew three times almost like someone wants us to go towards it. You're right Cross, but we already had this discussion earlier. Channing and I were going to check out the captain's deck while you three stay here and ran through the dining area again. In fact, wasn't it your suggestion in the first place to split up?"

Monroe sighs. "Still pointing fingers, I see you haven't heard a thing we said, have you? I mean don't get me wrong, it's only natural to be suspicious of each other when you get in situations like this, but it doesn't do any good. Only because this might be a first time for some of you, but I can assure you if you still want to be detectives this will not be your last. Now, as I mentioned before, I'm calling this simulation off, as we all realize someone is after one or all of us. So, in order for that not to happen, from this point on nobody here goes anywhere alone. To clarify we don't split up not even in groups, wherever we go, we go as the entire group. I don't think I need to explain the reason why, do I? Good cause if I needed to explain why then you chose the wrong profession. So, to solve this argument and tension in the air, we will all go to the captain's deck and go from there. If anyone separates from the group, we will assume you are the one's behind this, but I don't think he or she won't disagree with me. Does anyone here have a problem with that… good lets' go."

Keys sighs. "I know Rakes and I'm working on it, but in the meantime."

Rakes nods. "Yeah, I know… she can handle it… but I guess it wouldn't hurt if we can wrap up this case a little faster."

Island fever, what the hell is that about? No seriously, think about it. Just what is it? There have been moments in history where this fever has been known to reveal itself. If you're caught up on your history than those moments would be Croatoan, Clue or Ten little Indians. There are something's in humans that just can't be put under a microscope. Example; that six sense, intuition, or that gut feeling that we get when something is wrong. What is it… I mean you can examine, slice, dissect, and read all the books there is, but you can never put your hands on it. In all actuality its' what keeps us alive and to be honest and without it the majority of us would be dead already. It's the sad truth that I sometime have to tell myself in order to keep myself balance if you will. If ever such a moment occurs, I always tell myself which one can keep me alive? That six sense, that gut feeling… no we know that right choice often comes to that one… intuitions..

Monroe stares. "He already thought up a plan, in fact he might have one or two in already in motion somewhere? So, I'm pretty sure what Gamble said holds some truth to it, but I have to ask was what he said true? You already know who's behind this don't you?"

Keys grins. "C'mon Monroe, you've known me for a few years now, if I knew who that person was that's trying to kill someone, I would have been told you. However, I guess in this situation no one was technically hurt or was almost killed, just their pride and dignity. But of course, we don't want that to escalate, so we might want to get ahead of things a little faster."

Monroe scoffs. "Of course, but you still didn't answer my question. It's fine, I guess I should be used to it by now. It's as you said we've been partners for a few years now, and I'll always trust your judgement. I'm not too sure about Gamble and Rakes, but I know we're all thinking of a way out of this situation. But I do have to agree with him on some point, you might not want to wait too long on whatever it is you got brewing in that head of yours. There's an old saying that still holds true, you're good Hank, but someone here just might be a little bit better. This is the control room, humph even though I've never been in ship's control room before I have to say I expected it to be bigger."

Cross sighs. "Now there's some irony Lowell. Didn't you mention that you've been at this restaurant before? I find that hard to believe that you and your wife didn't at least do some sightseeing. If you were paying attention Cross, I already mention that this restaurant wasn't on a ship when I was last here. But somehow, I got the feeling that you were just trying to see if I would remember, still suspicious, are we?"

Ellis stares. "C'mon you two not now, we're here looking for anything out of place. I guess for starters where's the hell is that button or switch for that horn, so I can tear it out. Is that it, no what is this, why is this button flashing? Auto pilot… why is the auto pilot button flashing!?"

Westwood gasps. "Well, we are on a ship I guess it would be common sense, wouldn't it? There is only one reason for that, I think you all might want to look out the window. Please someone tell me that's some kind of projection screen or something? This is all part of this simulation right, because if not, I think we're in the middle of the ocean! I really don't know why but It's strange for some reason I can't say I'm surprise."

Channing sighs. "You know I think you're right on the not being surprise part. I get the funny feeling that our supervisor's already knew that, or am I wrong? I take it you are going to tell us that you are as surprised as we are?"

Gamble grunts. "Well look at you, someone has gotten a little more bass in in his voice. Why don't you tell us how you really feel Channing? It seems to me that something has been weighing on your mind lately. Care to share… no, then I suggest you keep your judgments to yourself. But to answer your bold statement earlier, it's more yes and no. In simpler terms we just found out ourselves not too long ago that this ship was moving. We just didn't find it all to relative at the time to catch everyone up, but apparently that has change. And even if we did find it relative to share with you five, we were in no way obligated to do so. Now that that's out the way, you all should be caught up, you now know what we know."

Cross stares. "I'm actually with Channing and Ellis here, for some reason I can't say I'm too surprise either. The only thing I want now is to stay alive long enough and get whatever this is over with. So, we're in the middle of the ocean, and possibly with a killer on board, what's the play here?"

Lowell sighs. "Well, being in the middle of the ocean does change things around here. For intents there's nowhere to run if we need to. I guess in a sense that would be the idea. So, I think we should hurry and get this search over with. Hey Ellis isn't that the switch for the horn over there, why don't you hit it? That's a horrible idea, why in the world would I want to do that? I agree with Ellis, that's not a good idea. For all we know that's exactly what the killer wants! That's a good point Westwood, but wasn't that the idea of coming here in the first place? And plus, I don't think the killer would lure us all here just to blow us up or anything."

Monroe sighs. "Look at that, now they are starting to think like you Keys. That's smart thinking Lowell, and I agree with you. In situations like these we have a nickname for them, we call them scavenger criminals. These type of criminals like to play games, it's a sort of rush for them when they think their smarter than the cops or a particular person. Case in point our current situation we're in now.

Keys grins. "She's right, scavenger criminals like to leave clues around the crime scene. It's annoying, but these types of criminals fall into two categories. The first is the ones who need some kind of validation for their crime, as Detective Monroe stated they want cops to know they are smarter than them. So, they play this game of cat and mouse scavenger... a sort of look at me catch me if you can. The second is criminals who focus on a particular person or persons for whatever the reason may be, normally it's some sort of obsession or revenge, I can say normally it's the ladder of the two. With that in mind I think we all can agree to focus on the second category of this scavenger killer. Now even though I just told you that, I don't want you to rule out the first type of criminal, the one for validation. Being a good detective means never trying and focusing on one type of criminal. Even if the evidence seems to point to that type of criminal, always keep your mind open. Having a closed mind can sometimes lead to tunnel vision and some of these smart criminal can pick up on that and use it to their advantage."

Ellis nods. "I see, well I think by now we all can agree that this scavenger criminal isn't focusing on just one of us, but everyone here. Well, I guess I should say almost everyone here, but still, I guess the majority still beats one person."

Westwood stares. "Scavenger huh… I guess that will make sense if you stop and think about all the things we found during this thing. Lowell's signature, Ellis and her crossword puzzle, my husband's meal, and Cross's pocket watch chain. Sounds like a scavenger hunt to me, but don't all scavengers have a point to them?"

Rakes grins. "That's what we're here for Westwood, to figure out the point of it all. The only hard part is trying to figure it out before someone gets hurt or killed. So, in order for that not to happen we need to get back on track and search this room. Remember what we said about this being a scavenger criminal, which means the unsub, if you will, wanted us to be here. So, we need to look around carefully and figure out what is not supposes to be here. And yes, I know some of you have never been on ship before, neither have myself, but just humor me and look around for anything out of place."

Channing points. "Will a small chandelier qualify as out of place; remember why we came here in the first place? Look… next to the ship's switch for the horn. I would say a chandelier would qualify and definitely doesn't belong."

Lowell grunts. "I say you're right, and again how did we missed that? Or I should say how did I missed that, this whole thing is becoming too exhausting. Do any of you all recall what I said about the differences between this restaurant and the one I proposed to, even though this is the same restaurant? We'll let me refresh everyone's memory, I mentioned there weren't any chandeliers the last time I was here. I'm not sure, but I think this was meant for me. Wait Lowell, you said you just forgot about the chandeliers, because you remember later on that you proposed in the red section… right? Easy Ellis

I'm old, I tend to forget things like everyone does. And plus, I didn't think I'll have to remember something like this here. So now what, are we back to pointing fingers at each other?"

Monroe sighs. "Not sure that was her intentions Lowell, I think she was talking about the color. If you can also recall, the dining area was divided up into sections. These sections were color coded by the color of each chandelier. Do you see where I'm going with this? Before any of you answer that question… Lowell are you just going to stand there or are you going to tell us the color of that chandelier? Oh of course Detective Monroe, I guess I jump the gun a little bit sorry about that Ellis, lets' see here… we got blue bulbs. Safe to say this came from the blue section of the dining area."

Cross stares. "The blue section huh, what's with the color thing anyways? Why would a restaurant be dividing up their sections in the first place? I don't think you ever explain that, Lowell. I'm not trying to point fingers again, but it is a logical question for this investigation. You want to tell us what's the deal with these things?"

Lowell smirks. "There's nothing really to tell, they don't really mean anything on their own. If memory serves, the chandeliers were the restaurant's gimmick if you will, something that sets it apart from other restaurants. The color coded was the attraction part that made this restaurant popular. I can't remember what color represented what section, but I do remember the red section was for special events or occasions. Case in point the section where I proposed to my wife."

Ellis sighs. "I see, so not only do these chandeliers hold some significant to you, but as Cross stated it would appear they hold some significant or has some importance to this case. So, since we found this one or better yet I should say, since we were led to this one, what would be our next play?"

Westwood stares. "I'm actually not too sure it's the chandeliers that holds the significant Ellis. Maybe it's just me, but I don't think we've answered Detective Monroe question. Its' not the chandeliers per-say that we should focusing on, but I think it's the color. You said there were four colors; red, blue, green and yellow right? You just mentioned you proposed in the red section, our Jane Doe was killed in the yellow section, and we have one of the blue sections chandeliers here, for a clue I presume. So, I assume the answer to your question would be to search the blue section of the dining area."

Gamble grins. "Well seems we found your counterpart Monroe, very astute deduction Ellis. And yes, before you say anything Rakes, I know what astute means. Anyways It's about time you all start acting like the top rookies of the academy. Although to be fair, you should have noticed it as soon as Lowell found that chandelier, but you are still rookies."

Channing sighs heavily. "I thought this simulation was over with, why do I get the feeling that you're still testing us somehow? Aren't we all in this together? In any case, I take it the next play would be to head back to the dining area…right? You would be correct sir, but before we do, hey Lowell do you remember yet what the colors are supposed to mean for each section? Or are they there just for decorations or what's the deal?"

Keys grins. "You know I always wanted to know that myself Rakes, it has been nagging at me for a while. As a matter of fact, you can tell us when we get there, I got a feeling that's not all we're going to find. We all need to be on guard, so stay close."

Ellis whispers. "Hey Cross, you think that was a good feeling or bad one? From everything that has happen today, I would say it's a bad feeling Ellis. But from what we've all heard about him, I think those feelings he gets have some merits to them, don't you think? Hey Westwood, you've been strangely calm, since it was your suggestion why don't you lead the search in the blue section. You don't have a problem with that do you?"

Rakes sighs. "Easy Gamble, I think you're catching that fever that's seemly been going around. We're all in this together remember. We're all searching that sections, for what I'm not too sure, but I guess we'll find that out in a few minutes. Humph… You know I never really notice until now, but this section is quite beautiful. No offence Lowell, but I think you should have proposed here. But that's just me, anyways so how about it Lowell, what's the deal with these color coded sections?"

Lowell stares. "Well as I mentioned before Detective Rakes, I thought they were the restaurants gimmick; I mean I've only been here once. It was actually suggested to me by my wife best friend. Thinking back and If memory serves, I know the red section was for special occasions and events such as wedding parties and big meetings. The yellow and green sections I believe were for your everyday customer. Only difference was in the yellow section you could smoke, and the green was a non-smoking area. I remember now because green was also refer to as the ego-friendly section. I'm not too sure about the blue section though, like I said before I wasn't really paying attention.

Monroe stares. "That's some memory for someone who wasn't paying attention. But base on the mannequins attire and champagne bottles on some of the tables here, I would say this is some kind of VIP section. Its' strange though usually you'll have groups of people sitting at these tables in VIP areas, but look at these mannequins, there no more than two to three people at each table. That's not the only thing partner, look at that table over there, notice anything missing? Yeah, out of every table here, this table is the only one missing a chandelier. So, I guess it's safe to assume that's where we're supposed to be led to? Alright everyone be careful and keep your eyes open for anything that looks suspicious."

Channing sighs heavily. "I have to say Detective Monroe I'm looking as hard as I can, but I'm not finding anything. Two mannequins with suits on and a champagne bottle are the only things I'm seeing here. There's the indentation where the chandelier was supposed to be. But judging on your faces you're seeing something we're not. Again, I thought we were all in this, but it's becoming more clearly that you know something we don't?"

Gamble scoffs. "There he goes again with the accusations, but you know I just don't have the time to argue or justify anything to you Channing. In case you haven't notice, we're in the same boat as everyone here, no pun necessary. In all honesty I was about to agree with you on not seeing anything here myself. Which got me thinking maybe we're in the wrong place so to speak."

Ellis stares. "I was about to say that myself. Hmmm what is it? You had that same look earlier, when you mentioned a bad feeling. You know something don't you, or are you just to keep everyone in the dark?"

Keys sighs. "The dark… I think you might be on to something Ellis. I might be overthinking here, but I think whoever is behind this made another mistake. Look closely at that indentation, it's been recently tamper with.

Which tells me that someone recently moved it. And there was only one window of time that could have happened. Does anyone want to guess when that was? When all the lights when out, and we heard that door open? So, what are you saying Detective?"

"Most likely what everyone here is thinking Lowell. During that blackout someone moved that chandelier and placed it in that room. Why…? I'm not sure yet, everything up to this point has been well thought out, but it's clear this wasn't premeditated. I do however have to agree with Gamble, I also think we're in the wrong place, or I guess I should say the wrong section."

Westwood stares with confusion. "The wrong section, but the chandelier came from this section, I mean there's the indentation right there. Why would someone take the chandelier from the blue section and leave it for us to find? And on that note, they knew it would lead us back here, but there's nothing here. This whole mistake, as you called it, seems to be pointless or just to throw us off the trail. This whole thing doesn't add up if you ask me. Simulation no simulation, revenge to scavenger criminal, killers moving around in the dark, and all the while in the middle of the ocean stuck on a ship. In all honesty a small part of me is wishing the killer would just get it over with, this is all starting to take its toll on me. I mean what the hell is the point here!?"

Monroe stares. "The point Westwood is to solve the case and keep everyone safe while you're doing it. Its' as simple as that, when you start to overthink about every little old thing that's when you start to make mistakes. Speaking of mistakes, I think we all can agree with my colleagues and saying we are in the wrong section. Even though we know this chandelier came from this section, I'm with you Westwood it doesn't make sense for the killer to lead us back here if there is nothing here.

Cross sighs. "I'm with Westwood here just give me my cigar and just kill me already. Humph I need a drink, I wonder if there is anything in these bottles? Never really had champagne before and if we're going to die, mind as well have a drink… why not? Stop don't drink that! Really Channing are you going to get on my case for drinking a little champagne? Barely took a sip, what's the harm? That's not a champagne bottle Cross… that's a wine bottle!"

Cross spits. "Where some water, someone give me some water! What the hell is this!? You want me dead, well I'm right here just get it over with. But really poison, I've have to say is not really my thing," breaks the bottle. "Now this, this is more like it, up close and personal was always a choice of mine. C'mon who wants it, I'm right here, how about it Lowell, or how about a certain detective who seems to be always two steps of everyone… c'mon I'm right here!"

Monroe stares angrily. "You need to calm down and take a breath! Your frustration is making you spiral out of control. Ok Cross, tell me, what are you going to do kill us all and then what? Case you've forgotten we're in the middle of the ocean. Can you drive a ship because I can't and how are even going to kill us all, I mean it's eight against one, you think you can do it with one broken bottle I would love to see you try? But, if you can, why not start with me, the way I'm feeling you might get lucky."

Rakes sighs heavily. "Detective Monroe is right on some levels, but you're not the only one here feeling pressure Cross. We all are in this together, don't get me wrong I guarantee you're not the only one here that is on edge. But if you calm down and take a moment to look around then you would see that this incident of yours could have happened to any one of us. Not saying anyone here would just pick up a random bottle and drink it, but it's not like that bottle has your name on it and said drink me! Even on that note there was no guarantee that you would be the one to drink it. So how could anyone of us set this up for a possibility on a chance that you would be the one to drink it, or any one of us for that matter?"

Lowell stares. "The detective is right Cross if you stop and think, it could have been anyone one of us. And plus, if you think back and remember our theory on Jane Doe murder. We said that we thought she was poisoned from the wine she drank, so why would someone plant this bottle here knowing that we know that? Just like what we thought with the ship's horn and the chandelier, seems like a little too easy don't you think? So do you mind, think you can lower that bottle?"

Cross scoff angrily. "I'll lower it, but I think I'll hang on to it, you know just in case, if you don't mind! I won't apologize for my little outburst, I'm sure everyone here can understand that. I mean after all it could have happen to anyone as we all agreed. So now that that's out the way, if this wine bottle was the one that poisoned our Jane Doe than why is it here?"

Gamble scoffs. "You're missing a part of that question, why is it here is irrelevant so to speak. It's not why is it here, but more so who put it here? C'mon rookies think, was that bottle here already when you all first started this so-called simulation or was it place there during that blackout? To be honest I couldn't tell you if it was or wasn't, from a distance and quick glance they all look like champagne bottles. So, I guess the whole question would be should we be focus on the why or who?"

Ellis nods. "I see, both questions do holds some meaning here. I can't remember if this bottle was here before from the start either, but it would make sense if it was here. It might answer the why part, I mean if I were the killer, then this section would be the ideal spot to put the murder weapon, so to speak. Think about it, you got a crowded restaurant, you need a quick place to ditch the bottle, why not in plain sight, it's good, after all we missed it."

Westwood sighs. "That's a good strong theory, but you're still missing the question Detective Gamble asked? Was that bottle here before or was it placed there during that blackout? I'm not too concern about the why right not myself, but the question that is burning in my mind and I'm sure everyone here is thinking this too, someone here put this bottle here. Doesn't really matter if it was here before or after the blackout, it had to been placed here by someone… so who?"

Keys sighs. "There it is again, that sense of fear and tension in the air. Now don't get me wrong that's good on some point, tension and fear does have its' moments, it keeps you on your toes and focus. It might sound wrong right now, but keep that sensation, it does help every now and then. Case in point, do you remember what we called this type of crime… scavenger criminals. With that in mind, it's not the who we should be focusing on, but the why, once we figure out the why to this game, then nine times out of ten the who comes to light. We were led to this section, originally, we thought there was nothing here, but now we know why don't we?"

Channing stares. "The wine… you're saying the wine bottle was the clue so to speak? I guess that would make sense, after all it's what we determine what killed Jane Doe in the first place. So, if we are focusing on the why rather than the who, then I guess the question would be why was this left here? I with Ellis and Westwood here, I can't remember either if it was here before all this or not. So should we just assume it was here all a long and go from there?"

Gamble scoffs. "I think we all can agree that it's not safe to assume anything. There are still a lot of un answered questions here and the only way to get those answers is to stop standing around and get this over with. You five do realize Monroe called off the simulation right, which means this isn't a game where we all just stand around asking questions. You're still missing the big picture here, as we stated this is a scavenger criminal, I don't really care about why or who put the bottle here, don't you think it's the chandelier that we should be focusing on? You beat me to it partner I was about to suggest the same thing. To be honest when we found that chandelier in the captain's room, I thought it would spark someone else's history. But I guess that would be a little too easy and expected."

Monroe stares intensely. "I'm not too sure about that Rakes, but I am with you and Gamble on the chandelier part. Nothing about this is expected, but I'm starting to believe that chandelier was. We need to keep looking around, maybe this chandelier isn't the only thing that we were meant to find."

Keys low sighs. "I agree, but I think we're in the wrong section. And I only think that because of process of elimination. I know I know, but roll with me on this, and stop me if I'm wrong. Lowell, you mention that you proposed to your wife in the red section right, because that's the section was for special occasions and big parties. Jane Doe was found in the yellow section, and now this chandelier, in a way leads us to the blue section. By process of elimination, there is only one section left right? Now again that may be a little too easy and expected, but if anyone else has another idea, I'm all ears."

Cross smirks and coughs. "Makes sense, even if it is a little on the nose, it's the only section we haven't check yet. Normally I'd offer a few of us to check it out, but as of now I'm not taking my eyes off of any of you, no offense."

Ellis sighs. "Why are you still on edge Cross, out of everyone here you're the only one with a broken bottle in his hand. Don't get me wrong I understand, having that does tend to ease the mind a little. But I would be careful if I was you, being the only one with a weapon does make one more suspicious."

Monroe stares. "Easy you two, Cross I can understand your caution, but Ellis does have a point. You still having that broken bottle is making this situation we're all in more tense than needed. I suppose if I asked nicely, you wouldn't put it down, would you? Didn't think so, honesty I wouldn't either, so here's the deal you can keep it, but you walk in front of everyone and keep your distance. That goes for the rest of you four as well. We're still in this as a group, but something tells me that we're reaching the end here. What makes you say that Detective, do you see something we've missed again? In a sense yes Channing, but only because it goes back to what Detective Keys mentioned earlier. What we all missed, a mistake was made and when mistakes are made by a criminal, he or she tends to reconcile that mistake pretty fast. Being a good detective, we don't want that to happen, do we? In the end I guess it's a win-win situation, this is all finally starting to wrap up. That being said let's search the green section and see what we find. Everyone keep your guard up. Cross, you lead the way."

Rakes and Gamble stare at Keys. "I know and she can handle it.

It's sort of ironic if you stop and think about it. Oh, I'm sorry I'm talking about what we are all thinking about… revenge. Why is it that in some cases, planning and getting some kind of revenge can take years to achieve, but when you achieve it, it only feels good for about five minutes? Isn't that some irony for you, how can something takes so long to get, but when you get it, after a few minutes you feel empty? Now I did say in some cases, but we all know getting revenge has different sides to it, but let's just focus on the majority. Revenge is one of a demon's greatest tools that can be used to almost perfection. A person can be consumed with getting revenge so badly that that's all he or she thinks about, all while keeping a straight face in public. Some can take weeks, other months, and yes even years, those are the ones that are acutely planned to the T. Honestly, getting that type of revenge only to feel good a few minutes then feeling empty the rest of your life, is a deal a lot of people are willing to make with their demons for perfection. But you and I both know, there's no such thing as perfect.

Cross coughs twice. "You alright there Cross, you stumbling a little bit? Case you haven't notice its' been a long and rough day. Not trying to be rude, but your focus should be worrying about yourself Ellis. That wasn't a threat just a stating a fact, shouldn't have to tell you this, but keep your eyes open."

Monroe scoffs. "Don't think I didn't notice that look of yours Hank. Its' not your normal thinking look you do. Not to mention Rakes and Gamble given me the side eye. What is it, you think I'm losing it or something? Doesn't matter what I think Monroe, it's what I know. And what I know is whatever is going on with you I know you can handle it. That's the same thing I told Rakes and Gamble, but can you blame them? They're just concerned about you. As am I, but like I said before whenever you're ready, you know where to find me."

Westwood stares. "So, this is the green section, why is this section closed off? And look there more mannequins in this section than the others. Hey Lowell didn't you mention this section was the non-smoking area? I ask because look at everyone's table, there ashtrays on all of them. If this section was for non-smokers, then why are those here?"

Lowell sighs. "I also mentioned several times that its' been years since I was here and I was only here once. I'm working from memory here plus, for all I know I could be wrong about this whole color sections or they could of change it since I was here last. They could have changed the green section for the smokers and the yellow for non-smokers."

Rakes stares. "No, I think you're on the right track with this one, restaurants don't usually change their gimmicks. Especially five-star fancy restaurants like this one, the gimmicks after all are what attracts the customers. Plus, you mention this area was also known as the ego-friendly section, right? Well green is the color for ego-friendly so I don't think they would change that. Be that in mind, I'm starting to believe someone wanted us to assume that."

Ellis looks around. "So, what are we looking for, what's the clue? Nothing is adding up with this whole thing. We're just being lead around, other than finding things from each of our past here, what's the point of all this. To me being a scavenger criminal, so to speak, sound exhausting and pointless."

Channing grunts. "I'm not too sure about that Ellis, I mean on some point you have to admire the time it takes to put something like this together. Other than the criminal part, it's quite impressive, but I guess it would be exhausting. Excuse me Detective Rakes, you mentioned something earlier. Something about assuming the color sections were changed? I'm starting to share that assumption with you. But what is the clue here, or is the clue the assumptions itself?"

Cross coughs again. "Well look at you, I was actually thinking the same thing myself. Only one thing that's baffling me, look at the table by Westwood, every table in this section has an ashtray, everyone but that one. Being a smoker myself I only notice because I always asked for one when I go to restaurants."

Westwood sighs. "That's a good eye Cross, I'm surprise I didn't notice it and I'm standing right next to it. Lets' see here… well that's not the only thing that's missing here. If you look closer these two mannequins are the only ones that don't have cigarettes' either. Stop me if I'm wrong, but I think this is supposed to be the clue that we're looking for. We're in a supposed smoking area, but these two are the only ones here that would appear don't smoke. Now why is that?"

Keys looks around. "We've might be missing an important question. You said supposed smoking area Westwood, I'm still not so sure about that. I'm thinking it's the other way around about what's the clue here. Here me out, what if these two manikins are actually in the right section and everyone else is in the wrong section? In a sense I'm thinking this section itself is the clue."

Ellis stares. "So, you think Lowell color section for this restaurant was actually, right? If that's the case then someone intently put these two mannequins here, to what, through us off the trail? In a way Ellis yes, sometimes when working on a case involving a savage criminal, the clues that we found can be decoys or just there to stall for time. Stall for time, what do you mean?"

Monroe sighs. "As I thought, don't worry Detective Keys has a hard time explaining the thing he does. I'll do my best to translate, there's one important thing that all scavenger criminals have to be careful and mindful of…time. Now I know what you're all thinking, time is obvious, it's what every criminal needs. In a sense you are correct, but dealing with these types, time has to be acutely on point."

Gamble scoffs. "Damn can't believe it took me this long to see it myself. To translate the translator, they believe our criminal is stalling for time. Seeing what I see now, I'm in an agreement."

Cross coughs again. "Is it me or do all you all detectives talk in riddles? I'm still at a loss, see what? Seeing something else, you might want to drop that bottle, Cross. Didn't you hear your partner Detective Keys, we had a deal, as long as I keep my distance, I'm allowed to keep it… for protection of course. You said it yourself and it's clear that someone here is out to get someone in this room. Best to be safe than sorry right, so why should I listen to you and drop this bottle?"

Keys stares intensely. "Heavy breathing, losing balance, excessive blinking and redness of the eyes, and not to mention that perceive cough of yours. All of these add up to one thing, wouldn't you all agree? You might want to drop that bottle right now, because if I'm thinking right, it's making you sick!"

Cross coughs and drops bottle. "Damn it… and here I thought I was being paranoid. I had that feeling myself but didn't want to believe it. Don't worry Detective Monroe I'm a man of my word I'll still keep my distance. I think that's best anyways, so for the time being I think I'll just sit here, don't really have the strength to stand anyways. Stop looking at me like that Ellis, I'm alright I just need to catch my breath. Everyone continue, just stay away from me. After all, you can never be too caution. Actually, this works in everyone's favor, at least you can rule me out as the killer, right? Don't think the killer would make himself sick, humph well I guess some killers would be that crazy to do something like that. Don't tell me you weren't just thinking that, Lowell?"

Lowell sighs. "Honestly, I'd be lying if I said that didn't come across my mind, can you blame me? If the shoe was on the other foot, wouldn't you think the same thing? In all seriousness, we need to figure out how you got sick. I mean you barely took a sip of that wine and afterward we saw you spit it out. So, if you didn't fully drink any of it, how is it making you sick?"

Rakes stares. "If I'm thinking right, the wine didn't make you sick, rather it's the bottle itself. Hey Gamble hand me that napkin. Looking closely when wiping it down… Yeah, it would appear the outer layer of this bottle has been tampered with, it's sticky with some kind of residue. My best guess some kind of neurotoxin. It's a good thing you dropped that bottle when you did Cross, doesn't look like you got the full dose."

Westwood stares with confusion. "So, you're saying someone laced the wine bottle, but why? Wait, so are we saying the wine bottle wasn't the clue for us to find in the blue section? Or rather the clue was the toxins on the bottle, but even that doesn't make sense. There was still no guarantee that anyone here would touch it or even drink it. Was this just another décor or stall tactic that you mentioned!?"

Monroe sighs. "One question at a time, you're starting to spiral. Now you could be right about the why Westwood, but let's focus on the who first. Yes, it could have been another stall tactic, anything is possible, but I'm not too sure about that. This, like everything else, was meant for someone. Remember we were led to the blue section, the clue we found, either being the wine bottle or the toxins on the bottle, they were place there, question is for who? We can sort of rule out Cross, no offense, but I don't think the killer would try and kill himself. Sort of defeat the purpose of him planning all of this if he's dead."

Ellis nods. "So that just leave the eight of us. Sorry Detective Monroe, but you did say we're all in this now, would be lying if I said I wasn't going to include you guys, no offense. Non-taken Ellis, I also told you all to keep your guard up at all times, glad to hear you're taking my advice. Please continue, looks like you got something on your mind. Yes, its' been on my mind for a while, we've been trying to figure out why and who put the wine bottle in the blue section right? But what's been eating at me was who was the wine for in the first place?"

Keys side smiles. "Careful Ellis, I might make you my protégé if you keep that up. I been thinking the same thing and I might have an answer to that question. Each time we found something, it was unique to someone here. The restaurant, the crossword, the standard meal, and the pocket watch. And now this chandelier that led us to this wine... question is who is this wine unique to? But I believe I'm asking the wrong question, I don't know maybe I'm over-thinking. Sometimes when trying to figure out those type of questions, it's always best to go back to the beginning. Who was it for... well if it's whom I'm thinking, then the only person it could be unique for is, your Jane Doe."

Lowell sighs. "Yeah, I can see that, after all it is what we thought killed her in the beginning. I can see the similarity, but that was just one of our theory's. It was the strongest one, but we also said that her wrist was slash and that it was made to look accidental. This whole thing is just theories upon theories, we still don't even have our why Jane Doe was killed in the first place!"

Cross coughs. "Isn't that what we're supposed to be figuring out in the first place? Wasn't that the point at the start of all of this? All this running around and what did we get, a dead Jane Doe and me being poisoned. Hell of a day for the top rookie recruits don't you think?"

Rakes stares. "Just take it easy Cross and catch your breath. You might already know this, and I hate to be blunt, but if we don't get you to a hospital soon Cross, then you could die. We don't know what kind of toxins were on that bottle and even though it looks like you didn't get the full dose, we can't play on time."

Monroe nods. "I agree, which is why we're all heading to the captains' quarters again. Every plane and every ship all have one thing in common. They all have a satellite phone for emergency usage, we need to find that phone."

Ellis stares. "Wait, what about you guy's phones, Sgt. Williams took ours when we started this thing. I'm guessing yours too, so not only don't you have weapons, but you're telling me no one here has a phone?"

Gamble scoffs. "You would be correct Ellis, the sergeant took our phones and weapons as well, said the realer the better. Whatever that's supposed to mean, some good that turned out to be. Honesty I'm sort of kicking my own self for not thinking about that satellite phone earlier. But it would appear we have a wrench in that plan of your Monroe. In case you haven't notice not everyone here can apparently move at the moment. I'm well aware of that Gamble, but we don't have a choice at the moment. I thought you would be the last person to complain about calling for an extractions and getting out of here. But that's not the hot issue at the moment If we don't call for help, then Cross will succumb to the toxic and I'm not waiting around to be the next victim of this charade. I know I'm breaking my own rule here, but I think we can agree the urgently. We split up one last time, four of us will head to the captain's quarters and the rest will stay here. Whoever is behind this, I think we can say poisoning Cross wasn't part of the plan. And even if it was planned, we all still need to keep our guards up, don't think no one here will object to that? Good, so this is how it's going to go, Westwood you, Rakes, Lowell and I will go with me and get to that phone. Keys you, Gamble, Channing and Ellis stay here and keep an eye on Cross, no offense again Cross. If it makes you feel any better, you're not the only one being watch, we all are."

Cross grins. "Honesty I'm not really surprise just as long as they stay their distance, they can watch me all day. But I'm not the one that needs to be watched, I suggested you watch yourselves. And that wasn't a threat or anything, just thought I state the obvious. Be that as it may, do me a favor and put a rush on making that call. I can't guarantee anything, but I'm getting a little numb in the legs, so I'm pretty sure I'm not going anywhere no time soon. Everyone set your watches for ten minutes, hopefully we're back by then. Alright hang in there Cross we'll be back as soon as possible."

Ellis stares. "Hey Cross you mentioned numbness in your legs, right? Is there anything else you're feeling? I don't think anyone here wants to know how I'm feeling Ellis. Just humor me Cross, my mom used to make me volunteer as a candy strip when she worked as a nurse. Didn't really like it, but what can I say I picked up a few things, so tell me other than the numbness how you holding up?"

Cross coughs. "Alright I'll humor you, the numbing is starting to affect my arms now to the point where I can barely lift them. It's getting harder to catch my breath, my head is starting to spin, and these lights are killing my eyes. Not to mentioned it feels like I'm going to throw up half the time. So base on that, what's my pyranoses doctor? I got a few ideas, but I'm not too sure yet. Do me a favor, you mind if I take a look at your hands, don't worry I'll keep my distance just hold them up for me, if you can. I can't really lift them at the moment, but I got just enough strength to flip them over."

Ellis stares intently. "I see, thanks you can relax now Cross. Excuse me detectives, you mind if I walk over here to the yellow section right quick? You don't need to ask us for permission, just as long as we can see you and we can see your hands. Not trying to insinuate anything, but can't be too careful, you understand right? No harm no foul Detective Gamble, I understand all too well. To ease some of the tension, Detective Keys can join me? I'm just heading over here to take another look at Jane Doe again."

Channing sighs. "I was thinking the same thing and plus if I stand in one place too long, I'll go crazy. Besides I'll be lying if I say that hasn't been weighing on my mind."

Keys grins. "Want to compare Cross symptoms to Jane Doe incident. That's a good idea and if memory serves you all never had a definite cause of her death, just several theories, right? I guess we got some time to kill, no pun attended, no time like the present. So, if you don't mind me asking, what are some of the theories did you all come up with? Well, if I recall right, we had three, I think. At first, we assume a domestic dispute, whoever Jane Doe was meeting gotten into an argument and she was pushed into the glass table. Well, I shouldn't say whoever, we knew she was with a woman at some point on the count there were two wine glasses. Second, we assume she was poisoned sometime during her meal and our killer took advantage and shoved her into the table. And third, we believe it to be accidental, she might have gotten drunk from the wine, stumbled and broke her heel and fell into the table. Either way we knew it had something to do with the wine somehow, but then Channing here had a different theory."

Channing sighs. "I wouldn't say different, but more or less all the theories in one. I just made the suggestion that she was poisoned, then shoved into the table to make it look accidental. For example; she starts eating and drinking her wine and then afterwards she starts to convulse. Our killer comes behind her acting like she's helping her and then with a little nudge, shovels her in the table. But there was a problem with the part about falling in the table. As you can see there are cuts all over her body, that's somewhat standard with a fall through a glass table, but look here closely at her wrists, see that, these cuts are parallel and precise. Now I know what you're thinking, but only problem with that thought is there's no blood, so she couldn't have bleed out, so why cut her wrist after she falls? It didn't make sense, so we went back to our strongest theory for the time being and that she was poisoned by the wine. Only because if you look there, the glass that fell with her is half full and the other is empty, so as it looks that theory seems to hold for now."

Keys stares intensely. "I see, all good observations and it's always good to go with the strongest theory. No blood… you're right so why cut the wrists…

it is a mystery. I guess that question can wait for now, I think we should figure out the main question first. You all assume it was poison that killed your Jane Doe, but now I'm sure we're all thinking something different. You're thinking the toxins on that bottle are what started the deed, am I right Ellis? Yes sir, it would appear that would be the case. The suited weapon choice for a female killer is majority of the time some type of poison or toxin. Poisons and toxins share a lot of similarity, which why it makes it hard to determine in a case like this one. We assume our Jane Doe here was poisoned, but when looking closer at her hand, she has a faint reddish whip across the inside of her hand. The same whip that Cross now has on his hand. I'm thinking when she grabs the bottle the toxins entered her system, killing her. The only problem with that thought is that we don't know how long it took for the toxins to actually kill her. So, we can't say how long Cross has before succumbing to the same thing. My best guess is a few minutes, maybe ten minute's top."

Channing sighs. "So that's why you asked Cross to show you his hands, so the wine bottle is still our murder weapon, but just not what we thought. It would appear we had it wrong then, she wasn't killed by some poison in a bottle, but rather the toxins on it. So, at some point Jane Doe here must have come in contact with the wine bottle and within a few minutes succumb to the toxins. That might answer that question on what actually killed her, but through all this we still don't have our why and even more important, how all this even happened!?"

Ellis stares. "Easy Channing, you're not the only one on edge, we all want this to be over with. Remember what the detectives told us, the why usually comes when we figure out the rest. However, we're still on a time limit, not for the simulation case, but for Cross. Judging by what I'm seeing, I don't think he'll last long."

Cross coughs. "You don't have to whisper I'm pretty sure I can tell what you're thinking. So, what do you think doctor, how long I got, best guess? Doesn't matter really, I can feel myself fading pretty fast. Guess I won't make to the end of this thing in finding out who the killer was. That's some irony for you, killed in a suppose simulation murder, and in the same way Jane Doe was killed."

Gamble sighs. "Hey save your breath, you need to conserve your strength! I'm sure by now Monroe and the others have made that call and help is on its way. Besides I didn't take you for the giving up so easy type. Don't forget we've been around the block a few times or more, so we've seen our share of people being poisoned, myself included. There's several technics on slowing down the toxins, the main one is regulating your breathing. The goal is when regulating your breathing, you can keep the toxins from reaching your heart faster. So that's what you should be focusing on and leave the rest to us. Call it pride, but I can never give up even when I get poisoned. But I can appreciate the advice so I will roger that detective, at least I'm not bored, who am I to complain. Just rest Cross and focus on your breathing. Alright what do we got, he's not going to last long, did you find anything new?"

Keys sighs. "More or less the same, but as far as something new, I got an idea or two. But before I tell you that, I need to check and confirm some more. Sorry again not trying to be difficult, but it's just my thing. There's one thing that has been nagging at me for some time, this whole thing was personal. The majority of you five had something personal tied to this simulation. Either something was taken, or you found something here that had a personal effect on your life. Which leads me to think, what was personal to our killer?"

Ellis stares. "We've establish that this was planned very well, wouldn't that make this whole thing personal. You said he was a scavenger killer, what if the things we found is a meaning or something? With any kind of killer, there is always some kind of meaning Ellis. Whether vengeance, or an obsession of some kind or just enjoyment, but with this I'm thinking all the above. We did get one thing right, this whole thing was definitely meant for someone, call it intuition but I'm not sure that person is here at the moment. And let me be clear, I mean here in this room."

Gamble sighs heavily. "Almost forgot myself, but you sure about that Keys, there's multiple ways that can go wrong and it will be on you. You're right Gamble, but as you can see, we don't have time to wait around, Cross is fading faster by the minute. Besides you should know me by now, and if not I'm sure Rakes told you my number one rule."

Channing sighs. "There you go again, leaving all of us in the dark. I thought we were all a part of this, what aren't you telling us now!? Detective Gamble you said you almost forgot, forgot what? And you asked if Detective Keys was sure about something, sure about what, what is it!? You all were behind this whole thing wasn't it!?"

Gamble scoffs. "I'm starting to like this guy, got a lot more bass in chest than before. Easy Channing, we didn't lie we just didn't tell you, and plus no one ever asked. If you stop and think for a moment and go back towards the very beginning of all this, it would become clear. We were your supervisor watching you solve a murder, but we weren't the only ones watching you. Get it now, It's the only thing that's starting to make sense, we were evaluating you, but someone had to evaluate us, right? Think about it really hard now, did anyone here even see him leave? I'll be the first one here to admit, I wasn't even paying attention. Think about what, see who leave, what are you talking about?"

Ellis stares with confusion. "I'm with Channing over here, I'm still in the dark, there were only nine of us here before all of this. Are you saying there was someone else here the whole time? That can't be, I realize this is a huge ship and all and I'll admit that we didn't check the entire ship, but in case you've forgotten we're in the middle of the ocean. Besides if there were someone here watching you Detective watch us, then they would have called this off after Cross got poisoned. No there's no one here, because if there was then Detective Monroe would never have had to go looking for that phone… well unless."

Keys grins. "Exactly, looks like you catch on pretty quickly Ellis, the only reason no one has called this off, besides Monroe is because they wanted it to happen. Well, I guess I shouldn't say they at least for the moment, but rather he. There's no point in continuing this charade anymore, had to realize we would figure it out eventually, so what do you say… sergeant!?"

Sergeant laughs. "What I say, is that you all failed! What I say is that I should have slit your throat when I blacked out the lights. I'm sure this is not news to you, but I really do hate you and that annoying thing you do that seems to always solve the day… case in point. But before you start getting full of yourself, this has nothing to do with you or some revenge, well maybe a little revenge. I know what you're thinking Detective Gamble, what are you doing Sergeant, why this and why now, and I can probably surmise you couldn't care less."

Gamble scoffs. "Well look at that, am I really that predictable, guess that's something I should work on. But in this case, you'd be wrong, you say all this wasn't about revenge, but what about Cross? If he doesn't receive help soon, he'll die and that will be on you. Or maybe that's the plan, I mean why have us in the middle of the ocean if not to kill us I assume one by one. Makes sense doesn't it, but if that were the case then why all the clues? Was this whole thing just one big game to you?"

Sergeant side smiles. "Humph, for someone who doesn't care you sure ask a lot of questions. I guess that is normal, when one's life is in danger you at least want to know why? Doesn't matter Gamble, in a few minutes we won't be in the middle of the ocean, we'll be under it."

Ellis stares. "What's that supposed to mean, are you going to kill us all!? What the hell did we ever do to you, if you got some beef with the detectives then don't drag us down with you! Why do we deserve to die, I don't even know you. In a sense you're right, but I wouldn't be too sure about that Ellis, no you don't know me, but in a way, I know you. I know all of you, your strengths, your habits, your hobbies, almost everything that is precious to you, I know. Ever since you five joined the academy I watched you. Before that, five years… five years I had to watch every last one of you. I guess you can call it my repentance for all I've done over the years. I lied, cheated, used people to get what I want and even killed. But ironically when doing those things to other people, some enjoy it, but when its' done to you… you ask yourself why? Like I said there's no point in getting into the details, let's just say what goes around eventually comes back around. Oh, excuse me I guess I was getting off topic now, wasn't I? Let's see where was I, yes five years, a year for each one of you I watched. Not so much as stalking, let's just say a skill of mine was hiding in plain sight. The biggest challenge was that I had to grease a few wheels and steer a few of you to join the academy. But luck was on my side so to speak, and here we are."

Cross coughs. "You sure like hearing yourself talk, but you're not making a bit of sense. Maybe it's the fading in and out on my part, but all I'm hearing is blah blah five years of watching, blah blah you lied, cheated etc.… As you can see, I don't really have time for that, but I am still waiting on that answer for Ellis question? I'm with her, I don't even know you myself, so again, why do we deserve to die?"

The sergeant says, "No you don't know me, but someone knows you or rather knows your past. If you haven't figure it out by now, this whole thing is your past coming back around… mine included. Why do you and the others deserve to die, sorry I can't answer that it wasn't my intention on killing any of you today."

Gamble grunts. "That's funny didn't you just mention that this ship is about to be under the ocean. And after that notion, didn't you say you wanted to slit Keys throat, but now you're saying that you have no intentions on killing any of us. You also said you've killed before, so what are you saying, you going to kill us without killing us? Lets' see if I got this right, if I were you and I wanted to kill someone on a ship in the middle of the ocean without killing them myself. Well, the only right answer would be, let me guess, you rigged the ship with some kind of explosion."

Sergeant chuckles. "And who said you were the slow one… ten minutes… ten minutes and then we all go under. Why so quiet Keys, I know what you're probably thinking and you're wasting your time. You think I didn't notice Monroe and the others aren't here, supposedly making a call to get help, right? Now I'm no mathmatalogist, but it doesn't take anyone that long just to make a phone call. I assume they're searching the ship to find that bomb and trying to defuse it yes? Doesn't matter they won't make it in time, you see this, dead man switch. What, you're not the only one who thinks two-steps ahead. So let them scurry around all they like, won't make a difference. Sorry Ellis, to me you guys don't deserve to die, but you know can't have witnesses. But I can say you all being here wasn't a mistake, pretty sure you figure that out. Besides I think it was for the best, you guys wouldn't have made good cops yet alone detectives. Other than not solving the murder here and running out of time, you all couldn't even get the basic information. Watching you all struggle with Jane Doe was painful, hell you couldn't even figure out her name. Well, we got a few minutes give or take, why don't we figure that out now, it would be a shame to end all of this and still not even know her name."

Ellis stares. "We were getting into that, but that's when the whole thing started with Lowell. Does it really matter at this point, honestly, we all wanted whatever this was just to be over with anyways. So, what's the point no one here is going to remember it anyways."

Channing sighs. "That's a strong word, and I think it would best fit this situation of ours. Remember… no one is going to remember, now I think that might be a little untrue. I think the sergeant is right Ellis, its' been eating at me for a while. What can I say I'm old fashioned. I like to remember names, especially from people that are precious to me. Call it an army thing, when you believe you're about to be killed, you would want to at least know everyone's name or the person that's going to kill you. Case in point, we all might blow up and even though our Jane Doe is already dead one of us might survive and just knowing the names of your fallen comrades makes it better somehow. Yes, I know it might not make sense to some, but trust me it does help. We figured out Jane Doe was assigned to the yellow section on the count the restaurant was color coded. But as Ellis mentioned didn't get around figuring out her name at the time. So how about it Sergeant, your closes to the hostess stand, mind telling us her name?"

Sergeant scoffs. "Well, look at you thought I was the one holding the switch and yet you're the one calling the shots, now that's a former soldier for you. Lets' see here, you said the yellow section right… looks like a few names reserved for that section. Mark sweets, Benjamin Moore and…what the hell… Breanna Williams! What the hell is this, why is my wife name on this list!? Move out my way, where is it I want to see that body. It…it can't be…the hair, her eyes, I've never seen these clothes, there all different, but it's her. This isn't the donor body that was supposed to be here, this… this is my wife! After all the lying, cheating and killing I've done I knew my end would come soon and I was prepared for that. But I was the one who was supposed to die not her! After all the years of watching and torture! I did everything you asked of me this wasn't the deal!"

Keys stares. "As I figured, it would appear that we aren't the only victims here. Solves that problem, Sergeant Williams was pulling our strings here, but he was just another puppet being pulled by someone else. We need to take advantage of this time and get that switch before he completely goes insane and just blow us up out of frustration.

Gamble grunts. "And how are we supposed to do that Keys, in case you've forgotten that's a dead man switch. If we attempt to charge him any type of way and he moves his finger we're all dead. He's got a point in saying even if Monroe and the others find that bomb, you and I both know neither her nor Rakes know how to defuse it. So, if you have something planned out as you mentioned, I think now might be the time to put it in play. This is just me at my best guess, he clams we got about ten minutes, but I'm assuming now we only got only a few left, maybe three, four tops."

Keys grins. "It's already in play Gamble. Keep both eyes open…focus… breath…remember squeeze don't pull and take it."

(LOUD SHOT)

The sergeant screams in pain. "Ahhh my hand! Damn switch! How's that even possible!? What the hell was that!"

That, Sergeant, was the second shot I made today that I would say was almost perfect. I don't know about that Rakes you hit your mark after all. Well in all honesty I was aiming for his wrist. I didn't know for sure if I destroyed the switch if we would still blow up or not. Guess you can say I took a gamble, but since we haven't blown up, I guess it paid off."

Gamble scoffs. "You guess… you gamble all our lives on a guess!? Since when do you guess? That's my thing to do stupid thing on a whim. And furthermore, where the hell did you even get a gun from and from the looks of it not just any gun, is that a rifle?"

Keys smirks. "Easy Gamble, sorry for keeping you out the loop, but I had to borrow your partner. Nothing personal, not even Monroe knew. You asked earlier if I had a plan in motion somewhere, that plan started just before that blackout. Just before we split up to start searching the ship, I had Ellis do me a favor and makeshift a rifle for me. Being a weapon expert has its perks, as you can see, definitely a hobby of hers that she mentioned."

Sergeant coughs. "How clever, would be lying if I said I wasn't surprised. What… you think this is over! Just because you've destroyed the control switch doesn't mean you've won. You changed nothing, this ship is still going to blow and being in the middle of the ocean there's nowhere to go. Have you forgotten that the timer is still going, all you did was give yourself a few extra minutes, if that much. You should just accept it, we're all going to die. I'm sorry looks like you were right my dear wife, karma eventually catches up with you sooner or later."

Coughs again. "Sooner for you and later for me, but in the end, I guess it's sort of poetic. Looks like you had a drink from your favorite wine before being killed. Humph, of course can't believe I didn't notice myself... that damn wine. Like I said before Keys, its' not over... you're not the only one who thinks two-step ahead."

The sergeant slits his throat.

"What the hell! He just killed himself! Why would he do that!? I mean c'mon do you think he was telling the truth about there being a bomb here? We're safe now aren't we, I mean it's over, right? Why is no one saying anything, is it over or not! What's going to happen now?"

Gamble grunts. "Would you calm down and be quiet? You're making my headache hurt ever worse. To answer your question Ellis no it's not over with and you would know that if you were paying attention. Have you forgotten about Cross over there? And furthermore, do you think the sergeant would go through all this just kill himself? Horrible way to go, but at least he was beside his wife. I do believe there's a bomb here, I just pray Monroe and the others found it."

Monroe sighs. "Well, you can rest easy Gamble, we found the bomb just in time and defused it. Well, I guess I can't say we, but him for that point. If you want someone to thank you can thank Lowell. No thanks needed as Detective Monroe said we just made it in time. Lucky for us all that my grandfather was in the bomb squad before he retired. He's the one you should be thanking, he taught me everything about making and defusing bombs. What happened here, we rushed back because we heard a gunshot? What the hell is that Sergeant Williams, his throat is slit, are you telling me he was the one behind this? Honestly, he wasn't even on my list of who I thought was behind this. No offence, but I still had my money on Cross, thought he was playing us. Can you blame me at one point I even thought you were behind this, but I should have assumed that, so I apologize."

Keys stares. "There's no need to apologize Lowell, I'd be disappointed if you didn't expect me or anyone here for that matter. It's not about trust, it's more or less instincts, sometimes that's all a cop has. Speaking of instincts mines telling me this isn't over just yet. There are a few things we have to catch you all up on, but for now we still have a murder to solve. What are you talking about Keys, what murder? From what I see Sergeant Williams was behind this, I mean he was about to blow us up before I shot that control of his. So, all we have to do now is find a way back shore so we can get Cross help, right?"

Gamble stares. "You're half right Rakes, the murder Keys is talking about is the one lying next to the sergeant. Who would have thought right, turns out the donor body was a real body, well you know what I mean? And that's not all, Jane Doe, is Sergeant Williams wife. To answer your other questions, no, the sergeant didn't kill her, he broke down when he figured out it was her. From what we saw I don't think she was supposed to be here. After discovering her. He went from calm and collective to deep depression and anger really fast. Guess no one can blame him for that, afterwards Rakes shoots the remote and a bit later the sergeant slits his throat with the broken glass from the wine bottle. Now you know what we know, the only thing left is the murder we started with."

Ellis stares. "This isn't a simulation anymore, that's a real body, don't you think that a job for you detectives to figure out? You just said Sergeant Williams was the one behind this, you got your scavenger criminal right there! It was clear that Jane Doe was already killed before any of us got here, so you know no one here killed her. If you ask me, the only correct answer for what to do next is find a way back to shore so we can get Cross help. I helped him slow down the toxins, but at this rate he's not going to last long."

Monroe sighs. "She has a point Gamble, that should be our first choice, but we still have a problem. We're still in the middle of the ocean, now I did manage to call the lieutenant using the satellite phone, but it'll be about twenty minutes before they can get to us. Unfortunate for us Cross doesn't have that time, I'm amaze he made it this long. There's got to be a first aid kit around here somewhere."

Cross coughs. "Thanks for the motivation, Detective. I'm sorry to disappoint you, but if I can help it, I don't plan on dying today. Plus, this isn't some cut or burn, I've been poisoned, and I don't think you're going to find an antidote in a first aid kit. No, I'll be alright, the breathing techniques Ellis and Detective Gamble taught me are doing their job, it's getting a little easier to breathe. Lasted this long right, I can last a little longer, also I could use the detraction and what better way than to solve a murder. Besides, I was awake through the sergeant's little episode of breaking down. He talked a lot about Karma, and it seems like he was trying to, I don't know, atone for his sins or something."

Ellis stares. "I wouldn't call it atonement. Well yes, a little bit, but it seems like he wasn't the mastermind behind this. After realizing his wife had been murdered, he said this wasn't supposed to happen and that it wasn't the deal."

Monroe sighs. "Because it wasn't the deal, Ellis. Now I'm just speculating, but as you just mentioned his wife wasn't supposed to be here. So, if his wife was supposed to be here, then the killer put her here for the sergeant to find. But even that doesn't make sense, the only ones who knew the sergeant was even here in the first place was us. Now I'll be the first to say the sergeant and me had our issues, he took my promotion for sergeant right from under me, but I wouldn't kill his wife for that. I don't know maybe this was some crazy lunatic and has nothing to do with us. Anything else, other than speculations before he died, did he say anything out of the ordinary?"

Gamble scoffs. "This whole thing is out of the ordinary Monroe. I mean why go through all of this just to killed yourself in the end. It's sort of clear that the sergeant was a victim of being played, but then why not go after the guy who was doing it, why kill himself? Maybe it was some type of atonement as you said Ellis."

(A helicopter approaches)

The best sound I've heard all day, finally we can get out of here. Hang in there Cross, you're going to be ok. So, what now Detective Rakes, I mean what happens to us?"

Monroe stares. "Don't worry too much about that Ellis. They are going to take our statements and as long as you tell them exactly what happen, everything will be ok. As far as the sergeant and his wife, it's clear he killed himself, but if not me and my colleagues then most likely homicide will take over it. I do want to apologize though for what all you went through. You get your first murder case, and you all nearly get killed. Also, on that note and it may not be the right time, but I want to congratulate all of you as well. There were some hiccups, but you all handle yourselves modeling well. Be that said I do want you all to keep this day in mind and let that weigh on your mind on what you want in life. As you know and can see, days like this for being a detective, come almost every other week. So you need to ask yourselves, is this truly what you want?"

Gamble grunts. "Well, you can think about that over at the bar when we get back. In my book, you all deserve a drink for what you been though, me most of all. Typical day for a simple recertification on a fake simulation, turns out to be a real murder and in the end all of us almost killed. Would I be crazy if I say I'm not really surprise? Guess I can say now I sort of feel what you sometimes go through… or am I wrong Keys?"

Whispers to Keys. "Silent are we, it's all good I'm pretty sure I know what you're thinking, or I assume I do. I'm not that slow, I know this isn't over, pretty sure there's a part-two to that plan of yours. This whole thing took years to plan, which means as you know there's an escape plan ready or already in motion when we get back to shore. I saw it too, that look in his eyes, pure anger with a little enjoyment. Just hope you know what you're doing, I'll loop in Monroe and Rakes after we land."

Keys sighs heavily. "Not just anger Gamble, I saw more of disappointment than anger, but in the end, there was satisfaction. And to answer your earlier statement, that part-two as you called it, will be ready when we land."

Rakes stares. "Hey looks like our ride is here, now we can get off this ship. I just hope they brought someone with them that knows how to drive a ship. The auto-pilot is still on and I don't think there's anyone here who knows how to drive a ship, is there?"

Monroe sighs. "Don't worry Rakes I've already requested a medic and a person who knows how to drive a ship. Only thing left to decide is who's staying on the ship and who's leaving in the helicopter? I know everyone is ready to leave, but we can't leave the bodies unattended, one of us has to be here for a few more hours. Don't worry, by us I was only talking to me and my colleagues, I won't make either of you stay another minute. Now obvious I can just tell you who will stay or leave, but I'm being nice… so?"

Keys grins. "Someone also needs to keep an eye on Cross. I don't know why we're dancing around this… I'll stay. You all get going, the quiet will do me some good anyways. Pretty sure we all knew that and besides… its' a beautiful day.

(THREE HOURS LATER)

Monroe stares. "Welcome back to dry land partner, how's Cross? I called before you landed and got an ambulance waiting. Also got crime scene here their waiting for us to release the scene."

Keys sighs. "He's stable, the medic was able to give him something to stop the toxins from spreading worse. He's passed out sleeping, so he's good for transport. As far as crime scene, there good to go you can release it. I assume everyone has given their statement to the lieutenant, other than Cross and myself?"

Rakes stares. "Yes, still going on as we speak now, the lieutenant and I.A wanted to talk to us one at a time before we got back to the district. They just got done with myself and Gamble, I think Lowell is with them now, and the others are over there by the pier."

Keys grins. "Good, well I don't know about you, but I think I'll go for a walk, need to get my land legs back. Be careful and don't go too far Keys, you still need to give your statement to I.A. Copy that Monroe, just going to answer a question that never got an answer to, I think they deserve that. Hey Ellis how's everyone holding up over here? I actually wanted to thank you, if you hadn't made that rifle, we'd been swimming with the fishes, so thank you that was good work. And that goes for the rest of you as well."

Ellis smiles. "Thank you Detective Keys I'm just glad it worked right, that was my third time making a rifle from scratch. And yes, to answer your earlier question, we're all holding up. Lowell and Westwood are giving their statements to I.A, I'm going in after them. As for the time being Channing and myself are just getting some air trying make sense of all things."

Channing sighs heavily. "Heard Cross is going to make a full recovery, that's good to hear. It's also good that none of us was hurt or killed in there. Simulation or not something like this definitely weighs on the heart. You guys are right, doing this job every other day and seeing what you see, it's commendable. Detective Monroe asked us to think if we still wanted to pursue this line of work and honestly… I'm not sure. I think we're ready Channing, me personally, didn't go through all that training at the academy just to give up on the first day at a crime scene so to speak."

Lieutenant yells. "Ellis, need you over here, you're next! Oh, guess I'm up wish me luck, and thanks again Detective Keys it means a lot."

Keys smiles. "Don't mentioned it, just when you get in there tell the truth and you'll be alright. I will, thanks. You know I'll have to agree with Ellis, I think you're more than ready Channing. You and the others handled yourselves quite well. I take it being in the army and around dangerous surrounding does help a great deal? I should know I was in the army as well and it does have its advantages. The things I've done and the things I've endured, it does keep one up at night. I don't want to bore you with the past, just trying to pass the time. Though if you think about it, the past is what started all of this. It amazes me sometimes what a person will go through just to get a few minutes of satisfaction."

Channing side smiles. "So you know… I'd be lying if I said I wasn't surprised. Your reputation does precede you and I'm not talking about you as a detective. Sergeant Williams and his wife are murderers and you born from a family of murderers, guess you all think alike in a way. Only difference is you're trying to make a difference and do some good, but the Williams's went in a different direction. But he was right in the end in saying Karma has a habit in coming back around. I planned everything down to the T, but as you know things don't always go as planned. No need to beat around the bush, you probably figured that out long ago. But you're right, this all started with the past and something that was taken from me that I can never get back."

Keys sighs. "Something precious… that is what this whole was about, taking away something that was precious. Ellis, you took her crossword. Cross, you took his pocket watch. Lowell and Westwood, well you took their happiest memory. The meal her husband has every year on their anniversary and the place of Lowell proposal. Can't get any more precious than that, but why the others? You said the sergeant took something away from you and I get it that's your business if you don't want to tell me, but why the others?"

Channing stares. "It wasn't them so to speak, more like their love ones. Westwood husband, Lowell wife, and Cross's grandfather, all of them played a part in my sister's death. After my retirement from the army my sister was the only one who held me together. We lost our parents when we turned twenty. So, she became mom, dad, teacher and best friend all in one, even though she was only two-minutes older than me. Yeah, you guessed it, she was my twin, and we did everything together. Few years later after our parents passing, my sister was killed. Naturally I'm enrage and wanting answers, but of course it was always the same answer. The cops are doing their job and we'll let you know when we have something. That something never came, the case just got tossed as a cold case of unsolved. As you know that didn't sit well with me, so I used what I knew and did my own investigation. And a little back ground on her, she worked with the mayor as an intern. So, you can imagine there was a lot of red tape for me to get pass, but it worked out. Anyways come to find out my sister was in the wrong place and overheard some things she wasn't supposed to hear. Corruption, bribes, or some kind of extortion involving who or what I'm not too sure, politics right? I only found that out because I was asked to come and identify the body a few days after she was murdered. The M.D said her cause of death was blood force trauma from falling down a cliff."

Channing smirks. "I already knew that was a blatant lie, my sister never did a day of rock climbing or hiking in her life. After everyone left the morgue, I snuck back in for a closer look. I broke in the doctor's files and found she had multiple toxins in her system, she'd been drugged. There were cuts everywhere on her body, clear signs she been tortured, but the ones that stood out were the ones on her wrists. They were deeper than the others, and that's when I knew. It wasn't blood force trauma she was tortured to death and left to bleed out. By now you can probably ascertain what happens next? Revenge consumed me for years until it became my life. All that I had left was time and patience and of course… hate. You asked why the others, well doing my time of investigation I found out the Lowell's wife was the secretary for the mayor, and my sister's mentor. I don't have any real proof, but I know she knew something. It was her job to look after her, protect her, but she chose her job over my sister. Cross's grandfather was chief medic, he was the one who signed off on my sister's death certificate. He took a bribe to falsify documents, money over someone's life how is that right? A week later after that, he had a heart attack. Westwood's husband was one the cops that claimed to discover my sister's body. Come to find out he was the who reported that my sister was killed by blood force trauma. Just another corrupt cop being used for money, but I guess in the end it came back on him. Few months after finding out about him, he gets killed. And Ellis found out that her father used to be an inspector and that he would look the other way when the mayor would, let's just say, make deals with certain underground people in order to keep his cozy little job. Just so happens when he was making one of those deals my sister was there and the inspector looked the other way for profit. About a month later he retires with his blood money greed and moves out of the country leaving behind a wife and our little Ellis. You asked why, well naturally I was going to killed the ones who were involve but Fate beat me to it, so I had to use next of kin and love ones so to speak. But all and all I couldn't kill them, Ellis, Westwood, Lowell, and Cross didn't deserve to die because of their love one actions. It didn't seem too fair, so I just decided to take something precious from them, a more of a reality check to always cherish what one has.

Keys sighs. "That's some story and you're right I can relate, being blame and used because of something a family member did. But still you're telling me you went through this whole charade just to teach them a lesson? No that wasn't it, at least not all of it. You said Sergeant Williams and his wife were murderers and he mentioned that himself? I take it at some point you must have figure out they were the ones who tortured your sister? I see, but a few things didn't go as planned did it, for one it was clear that he didn't know his wife was on that ship, he said it wasn't part of the plan. So, I take it you kidnap her or blackmail him in some way forcing him to gather information for years on the others for you to use as revenge? Am I on the right track?"

Channing grins. "More or less, the sergeant use to work for the mayor he used to be head of security. As you know that was just a cover, he was the one that clean and cover up certain messes if anything goes wrong. In any case you can probably fill in on what happened next. After tracking him down I forced him to do what I needed him to do in exchange for his family's life. That was the deal, plain and simple, he breaks that deal and I kill his family. Five years of watching the others gathering every bit of information from them is all he had to do. His torture came from only to be able to see his family once a month with a picture or two. But even planning everything down to a T has its challenges as you saw. I wasn't planning on him trying to blow up the ship and even worse I didn't plan on Cross to get poison. Like I said I only wanted to just squeeze their hearts, but not kill them. The toxins were meant for the sergeant not Cross. What… you probably asking yourself why am I telling you all this, basically incriminating myself for attempted murder. In all honestly I'm tired, I told you all I had that kept me going was hated and now that hatred is gone… all I have left is relief and exhaustion."

Keys grins. "I guess that would be the only thing left, but I think you missed something. You said attempted murder, you forgot murder too. You said the toxins were for the sergeant, but his wife was already dead. Not from the toxin, but from the way your sister died, you tortured her to death and made it look accidental as some kind of poetic justice. That got me thinking so I made some calls just before the shipped dock and after that I finally figured out the why. There were two-parts to why you did all of this and this is just an educated guess. The first was I learned that a few years ago Sergeant Williams had a sealed case on him. Turns out he was accused multiple times of sexual assault by multiple woman, mainly the ones he worked with. The case never went anywhere because as you know he has connections in high places. He raped your sister didn't he, something like that is definitely cause for revenge, I know I would kill him. That only answered half the why, the other was your primary target, the wife. You said the toxins were meant for the sergeant in yet she was tortured to death. It was clear you had more hate for her then the sergeant, so that got me wondering. A few calls later and some help from the medic I was able to figure it out, and I want to tell you before-hand, I may not understand, but I get it. Julia Channing, that's your mothers' name isn't it? With help from a few friends in the medical field I was able to get a file, your mother's birth records. Turns out she did give birth to twins… twin girls. Diana and Dana Channing, after learning that it made sense in why Sergeant Williams didn't recognize you. You mentioned he took something precious from you and there's only one or two things that a man can take from a woman. Something so precious that she has to change herself inside and out just to see him dead. It happened to you too didn't it, and at that time that hatred of yours was born. It might not make a difference, but I took out my ear piece before our conversation, everything that was said was just between you and me. Figure you wouldn't want everyone knowing your secret. Only thing left I have to ask before bringing you in is, where is his family and why the wife?"

Channing stares intently. "After learning who killed my sister I started tracking him down. Days to weeks, weeks to months of watching the sergeant and his family. I gather every detail waiting for the perfect time to make my move. About six months pass and I was ready, but I got careless. I was so eager to kill him that I didn't plan on the wife coming home early... it was just an unknown. She caught me sneaking around and blindsided me from behind. When I woke up she was sitting at the table, smiling and drinking that wine. With no other options I told her about her husband and what he did and why I was there, trying to appeal to her nature. I thought by us being both women and that she lived with him that she would at least believe some of what I said was true. I was wrong... do you know what she said to me while drinking that damn wine? She smiled and said I see it true, twins do share everything, you have that same look of fear on your face that she had. My face froze after hearing that, but the worse came later when her husband came home. I'll spare you the details, but to sum it up it was just me and him for what seems like to have been an eternity. I lost track of how many times he came in and out that room. And after each time he and his wife would toast with a glass of wine. Sick right... the guy was assaulting me repeatedly and the wife couldn't care less. Sorry I did say I would spare the details and you don't need to know all that. Needless to say as you can see I was able to get away and the rest you know. I got my revenge on the wife and made that deal with the sergeant. To answer your other question, I never kidnap the kids just took pictures of them to show the sergeant they were still alive. Other than hatred, protecting ones' family would be the only thing a person would do just about anything for. Before our conversation I made call to the person that was watching them, she dropped them off at the fire station earlier, there ok. Your partner was right and I see now what she was talking about. You definitely have a usual attraction and one hell of an annoying ability. But I don't think that will do any good at this point. I meant what I said before about being tired and I want to thank you ahead of time in taking out your earpiece. I knew you were a man that could be trusted with all of this and I can tell we think alike in certain ways. Be that as it may I can't let you walk away, I myself am prepared to at tone for what I've done and I'm ready for that, but knowing what you know I can't risk it. I got C4 strap to my chest, can't think of a better way for two former soldier to go out. I knew you would figure it out so I had this in the pocket just in case and even if you were to run right now you wouldn't be able to out run the blast. What was that notion he used just before silting his throat, you're not the only one who thinks two-steps ahead? I want to switch what I said earlier, I don't think that we think alike in certain ways, I know we do. I can just tell, you're tired too, so why don't you just enjoy this sunset with me, It's quite beautiful. But before ends, from one soldier to another I can give the respect and honor of my name, it is the only thing that we are given that is precious when we're born… I was born with the name Channing, Dana."

Keys smiles. "It's a pleasure Dana, but I never said I think two-steps ahead, that was just something everyone always thought about me. No, I said my number one rule for myself was to always have a contingency. I don't much like being almost blown up again for the third time in my life, it's really becoming a bad habit for some reason. And also it just so happen… I also made a deal."

(Loud gunshot)

Channing coughs and sighs. "Where… where did that come from…? Really the water? Who and how didn't I see it coming?"

Westwood comes up from the water. "No you wouldn't have. Detective Keys and I made a deal, once we figured out who was behind this, then the deal was, he was mine. And I have to say, he was a man of his word, this is for my husband you bastard."

Keys stares. "No Westwood the deal was that he was yours, but you can't kill him. You got your revenge and you saved my life, that's enough you don't need to kill him. Are you kidding me Detective have you forgotten what he did!? The pain he put us all through! I know Westwood you just going to have to trust me for now… please."

Lieutenant yells. "Everyone ok here? Yes sir, we're ok here right Westwood? Channing was on the verge of killing himself alone with me, before Westwood here shot him and saved my life. All and all it was just a flesh wound and everyone is still alive."

Lieutenant stares. "What happened Keys? Your earpiece cut out before we got the full confession."

Keys sighs. "Nothing happened lieutenant. Just a man consumed with revenge. The C-4 to his chest wasn't even real, he just wanted to spread some fear. My earpiece must have shorted out or something, but he wasn't saying much just the usual boasting and bragging to himself."

Lieutenant sighs. "Alright, well we got all that we needed from before the shortage, it's more than enough to put Channing away for a long time."

Ellis grins. "Seems like that modification I made for your gun to shoot faster under water came in handy Westwood, your welcome. So, Channing was the so-called scavenger criminal, was he? You're lucky Westwood, I think I can speak for the rest of us in saying I think I would have killed him. So how about it, Detective? I think we deserve to know why."

Monroe sighs. "In short, some criminals want everyone else to feel what he feels. Channing's whole thing was taking something that was precious from each of you. Try not to think about it so hard Ellis, the important thing is no one here was hurt. You all made it on your first day as semi-detectives and I'm proud of you all. Sandra Ellis, Lisa Westwood, Melvin Lowell, and I'll tell Eric Cross when I see him that if any of you decide to keep pursuing this career of becoming detectives, then I'll go to bat and put good words in for each of you. You never know one day one or more of you might be part of this unit. It might be for the best, some of us might not be here for long, you all go home and take some much needed rest. Have a good day."

Gamble scoffs. "Looks like someone nerves are still up, what's been eating her? That's a good question Keys, you keep saying she can handle it, but whatever it is, it's clearly handling her."

Keys sighs. "Yeah, I know Rakes, alright I guess you and Gamble got this here? Alight I'll see you back at the district. Even though you said you would tell me what's been bothering you once this was over, you don't have to do that you know? We all have our concerns, but whatever it is it's your business and I won't press it."

Monroe side smiles. "There's something I should have told you a while ago. When you were on leave and I showed up that day later at your house, well about a week later I missed my cycle. Turns out I was pregnant and before you ask, yes, you're the father. After that strip turned blue, my mind was flutter with chaotic thoughts. I'd be lying if I said that a certain thought didn't cross my mind once or twice. Should I tell him or just kill it, I'm ashamed that thought even crossed my mind."

Keys sighs. "There's no need for you to feel ashamed, with a history like mine, I'd be surprised if you didn't feel that way. So, it would seem you already made your choice because you didn't tell me until now. So why even tell me if you already chosen?"

Monroe sighs. "You didn't let me finish and I didn't choose, seems like fate had a different plan for me. Before this whole simulation murder happened, I got a call from my doctor. Turns out I had a miscarriage. You might not think so, but I was going to tell you because I actually wanted to keep it. Fun fact that you never knew about me is that I always wanted to be a mom. My regret was I didn't tell you once that strip turned blue, but not a single thought entered my head about you being a bad father. It may sound crazy, but knowing the little I know about you, I wasn't worried. Well anyways, that's what I wanted to tell you. Now I'm off to give my statement to the lieutenant. This day has taken its toll on me. Oh and do me a favor and keep this between us. Gamble and Rakes have really been nosey lately as if I hadn't noticed. Later, see you tomorrow."

Keys side smiles. "So, you're just going to drop a bomb shell like that and just leave? Can't say I'm surprise, if I were in her shoes, I would do the same thing. Humph guess I was right after all I wonder if I should have told her I already knew, not about the miscarriage, but I thought as much. I guess in the end it was her secret and she did tell me when she was ready. So, I guess it worked out and besides she would have most-likely been pissed if I did tell her I knew. Who am I kidding? I had no clue or maybe I did. I don't know, guess I'm just thinking out loud again, really have to control that."

To be quite bold killing is one of the easiest things to do when you think about it. Anyone can shoot someone, it only takes five pounds of pressure to pull a trigger. Anyone can stab or cut someone, hell you can make something sharp out of anything now-a-days. Poison, now that can be tricky, but if you know what you're doing then still highly achievable. The hard part is predicting "the unknown" of everyday life. One can't predict what a person is going to do, only anticipate it. Pulling a trigger, swinging a blade, or even poison are still the top deadliest weapons since the beginning of time. But without the deadliest weapon of them all, society wouldn't have existed. I am the key to failure, I am the key to victory, I am the key to everything and yes that includes history. All humans use me and even animals too, I can save, and I can kill so be careful, how you use me, well that's up to you: INFORMATION